Johnny stepped into the room and felt his mouth go slack

He approached the bed and stood looking at the still, unconscious form for a long time. When he turned, his body was as rigid as a plank.

"Will he live?" Johnny asked Dr. Volta.

"Do you know him?" she countered, evading his question.

"I understand he was asking for me. I was hoping he'd live long enough to tell me why."

But the doctor had seen the change in Johnny's face. "You know who he really is, don't you?" she said softly.

Johnny Bolan looked at the physician, then turned to stare at the pale figure on the blood-stained bed.

"Yes," he admitted. "He's my brother."

MACK BOLAN
The Executioner

DON PENDLETON's EXECUTIONER

MACK BOLAN

Hell's Gate

A GOLD EAGLE BOOK FROM

W☉RLDWIDE

TORONTO · NEW YORK · LONDON · PARIS
AMSTERDAM · STOCKHOLM · HAMBURG
ATHENS · MILAN · TOKYO · SYDNEY

First edition February 1986

ISBN 0-373-61086-6

Special thanks and acknowledgment to
Tom Arnett for his contributions to this work.

Printed in Canada

THE
MACK BOLAN
LEGEND

Nothing less than a war could have fashioned the destiny of the man called Mack Bolan. Bolan earned the Executioner title in the jungle hellgrounds of Vietnam, for his skills as a crack sniper in pursuit of the enemy.

But this supreme soldier also wore another name—Sergeant Mercy. He was so tagged because of the compassion he showed to wounded comrades-in-arms and Vietnamese civilians.

Mack Bolan's second tour of duty ended prematurely when he was given emergency leave to return home and bury his family. Bolan made his peace at his parents' and sister's gravesite. Then he declared war on the evil force that had snatched his loved ones. The Mafia.

In a fiery one-man assault, he confronted the Mob head-on, carrying a cleansing flame to the urban menace. And when the battle smoke cleared, a solitary figure walked away alive.

He continued his lone-wolf struggle, and soon a hope of victory began to appear. But Mack Bolan had broken society's every rule. That same society started gunning for this elusive warrior—to no avail.

So Bolan was offered amnesty to work within the system against international terrorism. This time, as an official employee of Uncle Sam, Bolan wore yet another handle: Colonel John Phoenix. With government sanction now, and a command center at Stony Man Farm in Virginia's Blue Ridge Mountains, he and his new allies—Able Team and Phoenix Force—waged relentless war on a new adversary: the KGB and all it stood for.

Until the inevitable occurred. Bolan's one true love, the brilliant and beautiful April Rose, died at the hands of the Soviet terror machine.

Embittered and utterly saddened by this feral deed, Bolan broke the shackles of Establishment authority.

Now the big justice fighter is once more free to haunt the treacherous alleys of the shadow world.

In memory of the 329 passengers and crew
of Air India Flight 182,
which plunged into the North Atlantic off Ireland
after an apparent terrorist bomb blast, June 1985.

PROLOGUE

Mack Bolan knew he was dying. The two 9 mm Kurz bullets had struck him in the shoulder. Weakened by blood loss, he had cursed the mental lapse, distraction, whatever, that had placed him in the path of the slugs. There was no time for self-recrimination, and Bolan had dismissed it, trying hard to concentrate on his erratic driving.

He had pushed his battered wheels almost nonstop until he had crossed the U.S. border into British Columbia.

Three days had passed, and the wounds were infected and Bolan's temperature was approaching the danger point. Only the warrior's superb physical condition had carried him along this far. Medical treatment might still save his life, but he knew that if he stopped, his pursuers would corner him for sure.

And that would mean the end. Despite his agony and general debility, the Executioner couldn't help wondering wryly which would get him first: his implacable trackers or the bullet wounds.

Many times before in his Everlasting War the warrior had expected this moment. And always he had eluded the grim fates.

Uh-uh, the soldier thought, as his glazed eyes took in the dashboard of the ten-year-old station wagon he sat in and the dismal surroundings of Vancouver's skid row.

Not here, he prayed to an unforgiving Universe, not like this.

His combat blacksuit had been abandoned with a minimum of questions the first time he had received first aid. He now wore only a red shirt and blue jeans. The Beretta 93-R was concealed inside the shirt, stuck in his waistband. The clothing and an army-surplus gray blanket were not sufficient to control the shivering that racked his body.

His tongue felt swollen, thick in his mouth, threatening to cut off each intake of oxygen with every ragged breath he drew. And no matter how he tried he could not seem to produce any saliva to help slake the thirst that made his throat dry, raw.

He experienced a sinking feeling, plummeting into blackness, but just as quickly surfacing to reality when it seemed that the void would engulf him.

Each time he touched the edges of consciousness, images flashed across his mind and he perceived figures waving to him, beckoning the warrior to join them. He made out the face of April Rose clearly and it confused him, because in his fevered mind he was sure that she had loved him.

"No, no!" he heard himself scream with effort, his shoulder throbbing with each word. Why are they calling me, the soldier wondered. I have so much still to do.

Hazy forms shifted in and out of focus and Bolan felt fear. The men hunting him were faceless now, but their taunts and jeers, indeed their presence closing in on him, made the weakened warrior frightened. Was this the way they felt, those hollow straw men who fell under the Bolan guns?

Come on, Mack, you can't lose it now, he admonished himself as he struggled with the vehicle's door handle. The latch surrendered and he slipped an unsteady leg onto the pavement. He pushed himself away from the station wagon and flattened his back against the alley's wall.

The sudden change in position further diminished an already dwindling circulation and the soldier was overcome by waves of nausea. He felt himself freefalling and saw the ground rushing up to meet him, felt it smash into his forehead and all was darkness.

1

Bolan found himself lying next to a trash can in an alley. The pain and warmth in his shoulder told him his wound had opened and was discharging blood and pus. He slowly unfastened his shirt and peeled it back. He desperately needed something clean to press against the wound to seal it again. He looked around, his eyes bright with fever and desperation.

He saw a newspaper box on the sidewalk. Bolan staggered out of the alleyway and was relieved to find that an American quarter opened the box. He retraced his steps, oblivious to the curious glances of the evening rush-hour pedestrian traffic.

Back in the alley with his newspaper, he extracted a few inside pages and folded them into a compress. Then he placed it carefully over the wounded shoulder, rebuttoning the shirt to hold it in place. He had to clamp his left hand over the wound to stop the bleeding through the paper.

Bolan was aware he was attracting attention as he staggered down the street. The sight of a government-owned liquor and wine outlet gave Bolan an idea. He went into the store just as it was closing for the day. One of the employees looked at the unshaven, gaunt, staggering form and automatically reached for their cheapest wine, the biggest seller in that part of town. Bolan squinted to focus his eyes on the list of spirits. He finally saw what he wanted and carefully wended his way to the counter. "I'll take that and a bottle of pure alcohol," Bolan told the clerk.

Expressionlessly, the clerk reached for a fifth of the clear, white spirit. Bolan paid the cashier with an American ten-dollar bill. The man carefully figured the exchange before giving Bolan his change. Bolan scooped it into his pocket without counting, put the strong brown paper bag containing the two bottles under his arm and staggered out the door, past the clerk waiting to lock up.

It took Bolan a little while to find another alley suitable for his purpose. He peeled back his shirt and took off the blood-soaked newspaper. Then, gritting his teeth, he poured the alcohol on the raw wound. It was like massaging his shoulder with a blow torch. Then he poured some of the alcohol on the newspaper and put it on top of the wound, put the rest of the newspaper on as a pad, and rebuttoned his shirt. It would help some. He'd have to find medical help within hours.

He opened the wine and swished his mouth with it and spit it out. He sprinkled a little on his shirt and tossed the rest of the bottle into the garbage can. The half-full bottle of ethyl alcohol went back into the bag and he crimped the bag around the bottle's neck. Now he was right for the part of a down-and-out alcoholic.

When he tried to ask directions to Jackson Street where he hoped to find his brother, Johnny, passersby assumed he was trying to panhandle. A couple gave him quarters, but would not listen to his questions. Finally, a teenager listened and gave Bolan instructions to reach the address he had for Johnny. Fortunately for Bolan, the address was only a few blocks away. A few blocks seemed like twenty miles, but he took a deep breath and proceeded.

The house was near the Chinese section of the city. It was one of a row of three-story, identical houses with front porches. The eight steps up to the veranda looked almost insurmountable, but Bolan took a deep breath and then placed his foot on the first step. It seemed to be undulating. One step at a time he fought his way up the steps and across the wooden floor of the veranda. He pounded on the door, oblivious of the doorbell right by his hand.

The door was answered by a girl who looked to be about fourteen. Her unkempt blond hair hung long and straight down her back. The blue eyes which should have been beautiful looked dull and uninterested.

"Got to see Johnny," Bolan gasped.

"He's not here."

"Got to see Johnny," Bolan repeated, unable to think of anything else, unable to formulate an intelligent response to the girl's comment.

Then the world spun and as much as he fought against it, he teetered toward the dead-looking blonde and fell into the doorway, the threadbare carpet coming up at his face.

2

Bolan had died and gone to hell. He had been pierced by a spit and was being turned over hot coals. Every now and then, one of the minor devils would dump a shovelful of the embers on Bolan's shoulder. He moaned, but he would not scream.

"Roll him over," commanded an imp with an intriguing female voice. "His wallet's probably in his back pocket."

Suddenly someone plunged a white-hot poker deep into Bolan's shoulder, penetrating his whole chest and gut. That forced Bolan to open his eyes.

A tall youth about eighteen years old was trying to roll Bolan over by pulling on his right arm. The pain was so excruciating that to Bolan it felt as if his arm was being pulled out of his wounded shoulder. Through watery eyes, Bolan could see the truncated tips of Western boots right in front of his nose. Above them, tight jeans seemed to stretch forever until they reached a white cowboy shirt with mother-of-pearl buttons.

Hands were pushing into his back, one forcing him to roll while the other explored his pockets. They were small, quick hands, woman's hands.

Bolan had managed to get rid of the Beretta's armpit sheath soon after he was shot. Now he tugged the 93-R from his waist and waved it until the snout pointed somewhere in the direction of the large belt buckle that adorned the tight jeans.

"Shit. Syndicate!" the male said.

He let go of Bolan's arm as if he could feel the fire flowing through it from the shoulder. Bolan rolled back on the hands that had been pushing on his back, trapping both hands and forearms under his back.

The girl who had been trying to take his wallet was forced forward, her head coming to rest on Bolan's stomach. Her face was hidden by the curtain of long greasy hair.

"Let me loose, damn it," the voice under the hair said.

As the girl struggled to pull her arms out from under Bolan's hip and shoulder, he spared a quick glance to take in his surroundings.

He was on a mattress on the floor of a large room. The windows looked out on houses across the street. The room was high-ceilinged and about twenty-by-thirty feet. Bolan's wasn't the only mattress; mattresses carpeted the whole floor except in front of the door. Mattresses were the only furniture in the room except for a table holding a film projector. The table stood on bare floor near the doorway. On the opposite wall, an oblong of highly reflective white paint had been applied right over the ancient wallpaper. It probably made an acceptable movie screen, but it seemed to Bolan to be low on the wall.

Bolan shifted his attention to the male, who seemed impossibly tall from Bolan's viewpoint. The head above the cowboy shirt was enclosed in blond hair that just touched the shoulders. Unlike the girl's hair, it was well kept and shining. The face framed by the helmet of yellow hair was the face of a teenager. If Bolan had been shown a photograph of only the head, he would have placed the age at fourteen or fifteen.

The teenaged girl finally freed her arms and stood up between Bolan and the wall. Her jeans were even tighter than the youth's. She wore a plain white T-shirt with nothing underneath. She would have had a good figure, if she weren't underweight and ill-nourished. Her shoes, nothing but thin high heels with straps, made walking on mattresses difficult as she picked her way around Bolan to stand beside the boy.

As she pulled herself straight, Bolan got his first good look at her. The golden hair framed an oval face, a perfect complexion and blue eyes. It might have been the face of a thirteen-year-old if the eyes didn't look as if they'd been around for thousands of years. Bolan recognized those eyes; they were the eyes of someone whose body walked the earth, but whose mind was already living the torments of hell.

Those eyes shocked Bolan to full attention. She was much too young to have been claimed by hell.

"We didn't know you were anybody," the girl said in her little-girl voice. "We just thought you were some wino who collapsed. We brought you in here and then were looking for...for identification.

"Johnny..." Bolan whispered. "Where's Johnny Gray?"

The two young people looked at each other. They seemed surprised that Bolan would ask for Johnny Gray.

"I told you there was something phony about him," the man said. "He's Mob."

The girl had more brains than to engage in speculation about the Mafia in front of someone she thought was a member of the organization. Instead, she returned to Bolan's question.

"He's not here right now. He probably won't be back until this evening."

Bolan was puzzled by these two. Why did the presence of a gun make them assume he was Mafia? Why did they take the Mafia as an everyday fact of life? And what was Johnny doing in a place like this.

Bolan gazed around the room again. The two were still showing signs of fear at having been caught going through his pockets. They stood in front of his gun, barely breathing, waiting nervously to see what would happen.

"Who are you?" Bolan asked.

The two young people exchanged glances. It was an unexpected question.

"Melody Megrims," the girl replied. Her voice was surly, the words mumbled.

"I'm Edgar Twichen. I'm an actor with Lion's Gate Productions." He said it as if the name of the company should mean something to Bolan.

If the pair before him had not already brought up the subject of the Mob, Bolan would not have made the connection. The only actors the Mafia was interested in did porn films. The profits from porn were rapidly rivaling gambling as a source of Mob money.

"You're proud of that?" Bolan asked.

Twichen grinned. "Best job in the whole damn world." He said it as if he meant it.

Bolan lowered the Beretta before telling them, "Sit down."

They cautiously settled down on the mattresses about ten feet from Bolan, trying hard to meet his feverish gaze and failing.

"I guess we better," Twichen said. "You passed out in the doorway and we had a hell of a time dragging you in here. I don't suppose you can get up?"

"I guess I'll have to wait here for Johnny," Bolan conceded, ignoring the query. "Is there any chance of finding something to eat?"

The girl looked at him for some seconds before replying, "There's some soup on the stove. Would you like some?"

Bolan nodded.

She turned to her companion. "Will you have some, Edgar?"

The youth ignored her.

Megrims shrugged, got up and left the room.

Twichen felt forced to confront the unspoken disapproval of the wounded, unshaven, unbathed man with the icy blue eyes who lay helpless on a mattress in front of him.

"What's wrong with the way I earn a living?" Twichen's voice had the aggressive note of someone who doesn't know whether or not he can confront the answer to his question.

"You tell me."

"Hell, there's nothing wrong with it. Not too much work, lots of money and all the good-looking chicks I can screw. What more could a man ask?"

"Perhaps for something useful to do with his life."

"What are you? Some kind of preacher turned bum? Why look down on me? You're the one who's about to have lunch with a cheap whore."

Melody Megrims entered during Twichen's outburst. She was carrying a tray that held heavy, restaurant-style bowls filled with a thick soup. Chunks of meat and potato stuck out of the dark broth. There was a pile of dark rye bread on the tray.

"You're wrong again," she told Twichen. "I'm not cheap; I'm very expensive. Have you told our guest about the super set they built just for you?"

"Go to hell, slut," Twichen muttered. Megrims stood calmly while Bolan painfully pushed himself up and around until he sat slouched, his back supported by the wall. Even through his pain and the enervation brought on by infection, Bolan could not help but focus on this woman. If her hair were black and her face held some life, she would look something like his dead sister.

Her calmness brought another comparison to Bolan's mind. April Rose, another corpse in the litter of his conscience. Passionate, fiery April would not have stood quietly while anyone fought for his life. She was alive, vibrant still in Bolan's fevered mind.

When Bolan finally had himself propped up, Megrims handed him his soup and placed the plate of bread where he could reach it. She then sat cross-legged within reach of the bread, facing Bolan.

"You bring me anything?" Twichen demanded.

"No," she replied.

Then she picked up the conversation with Bolan. "They built a special set for Hunk Jr., here. The bed's nine feet long and six feet wide and everything else is to scale. That's the only way they can use his only asset—his extremely youthful good looks."

"Lay off," Twichen muttered.

Bolan was impressed in spite of himself. He smiled, encouraging the girl to continue.

"Lay off, slut," Twichen repeated, voice sullen.

"You shouldn't have called me cheap," she answered in her little-girl voice. "I make big money, too, and for the same reason."

She turned back to Bolan. "The set is extra large to make Eddy look extra small. He's the biggest male star of kiddy porn. It's his lovely baby face. Unfortunately it gets harder and harder to find little-girl leading ladies who are five-foot-ten and look eleven or twelve years old. I'm afraid our star's going to have to graduate to adult porn soon. It'll mean a big cut in wages, but that's show biz."

"You a star, too?" Bolan asked. He sensed that the question was expected. The real question that was burning the back of his fevered brain was: What in the name of the Universe was Johnny doing here?

The porn star had a nasty laugh, but Megrims answered before he could speak. "No. I tried it, but I couldn't even fake it in front of all those people and under those bright lights. I'm a whore, like Eddy says, but I'm not cheap. As long as I can look underage, the Mob can get five hundred a night for my services."

"If you earn so much, Miss Big Shot, how come you never have any money?" Twichen demanded.

Bolan could see that Twichen was shaken up that a prostitute earned much more than he did. Bolan sensed that the boy really sold himself cheap. Why?

"Mind your own business," she flared at Twichen.

The star of kiddy porn snickered. Then he looked up and his evil chuckle stopped dead. Bolan followed his glance to the door.

The man in the doorway was dressed in a business suit. But the Executioner had been around his kind for too long to mistake the pedigree. To Bolan, he spelled Mafia. Whether he pronounced it Mob, Syndicate or Cosa Nostra, it amounted to the same thing—jackal man preying on the defenseless members of the honest community. And no matter how he pronounced it, the gun in his hand would shoot real .45s.

3

The most noticeable thing about the new arrival was his stainless-steel automatic. Bolan recognized it as a Wildey, a .45 Magnum with interchangeable barrels. This one had an eight-inch ribbed barrel that Bolan knew was capable of grouping all eight .45 Winchester Magnum bullets in an inch-and-a-half circle at twenty-five yards.

The mobster stood a little over six feet tall. His black hair was carefully trimmed and had just the right touch of gray at the temples. The skin had a healthy, executive tan. However, sun lamps and careful barbering could not hide the predatory animal that lurked behind the brown eyes.

Bolan, an expert on role camouflage, could see this mobster did not quite have the role perfected. Whoever he was, he tried hard, but didn't have enough savvy to get the role exactly right.

The hooker, Melody Megrims, was the first to recover from the surprise. She spoke to the stranger as if she didn't notice the gun in his hand.

"Hello, Mr. Hanchovini. Is there anything I can do for you?"

Bolan was at a complete disadvantage. He had the bowl of soup in one hand and the spoon in the other. The moment he opened either hand to try for a weapon, he was dead. His hands froze, but his mind raced like a Formula-1 engine.

The name Hanchovini plus the mobster's almost impeccable dress were all the clues Bolan needed. His computer mind raced through his Mafia files, collecting small bits of information, putting them together with the clues dropped by the two teenagers, until he had a connection. Frank Hanchovini, better known as Frankie Hanky, was a specialist in prostitution and pornography for the Mob.

The last Bolan had heard, Frankie had been the chief lieutenant of a *capo* by the name of Rodolfo Schizzetto, whose five-foot-three-inch height bought him the Mafia nickname, "Little Squirt."

Schizzetto was known as a provider of *provimi*, the Italian name for milk-fed veal. And the young veal he provided was in the form of young girls who were sold to flesh merchants and to those who were high enough in the Mafia hierarchy to be able to indulge particularly depraved and expensive habits. Things had become too hot for Little Squirt in Hollywood after he had almost succeeded in procuring two well-known juvenile actresses.

Two witnesses had been killed, even while the FBI had the Mob under surveillance. Then Schizzetto had disappeared but the porn and smut continued to appear. Bolan considered it a good gamble that Vancouver was Schizzetto's new base of operations.

"What the hell's going on here?" Frankie Hanky growled. The deep street voice and street accent shattered his respectable appearance.

"Nothing, Mr. Hanchovini, we just—" Megrims began.

Bolan interrupted before the young prostitute could give him away. "Hi, Frankie, how's the *pelli molle* business?" Bolan used the Italian slang "soft skin" to refer to supplying children for prostitution.

"Who the hell are you?" Frankie Hanky demanded.

Bolan had to force himself to concentrate, to dismiss from the back of his mind the constantly nagging questions about how Johnny had become involved with these people.

"I'm C.C. I'm here to collect my marker from you and Little Squirt."

"And who the hell's C.C?" Frankie Hanky demanded.

"Don't play cute with me," Bolan snapped back. "Corsaro Cancellari. I did garbage detail for Roman DeMarco. I hauled away Schizzetto's garbage when you two moved out of Frisco."

Bolan's story wasn't one hundred percent safe, but it would be difficult to check at this point. Roman DeMarco and his whole organization had succumbed to one of the Executioner's blitzes in California. As the witnesses disappeared a couple of days after Little Squirt and his lieutenant, Frankie Hanky, had gone to ground, the chances were good that they didn't know who were actually responsible for the murders.

Hanchovini was not easily sold. The gun remained pointed at Bolan's head.

"Says you. What the hell are you doing here?"

"Officially or unofficially, Frankie?" Bolan's voice took on tones of tolerant amusement.

"Whadda you mean, 'officially or unofficially'?" Hanchovini wasn't bright but he knew how to continue to bore to the point.

Bolan had no idea what he meant, himself. His fever was high, his thinking muddled. Responses were being dredged from deep inside his subconscious, automatically, based on a thousand other experiences of learning how to survive when pitted against the Mob. He needed breathing room at any cost.

Bolan let his voice grow icy cold. "If Schizzetto has to ask that question, he'd better ask New York."

The mobster blinked a few times, trying to assimilate Bolan's change of tone. Unable to decide what to do with this stranger, Hanchovini decided it was time to pass the whole mess up the line.

"You better come along and tell Mr. Schizzetto yourself," Frankie growled.

Bolan took two more spoonfuls of soup before answering, "I'm having lunch, Frankie. If Schizzetto's crazy enough to argue with New York, let him argue. It ain't my place to answer questions." He paused to take some more soup. After he'd let the mobster fidget for thirty seconds, Bolan gave him a malicious grin. "If Rodolfo really doesn't know why I'm here, then he'd better take it up with the bosses. They don't like it when I go around answering questions."

Frankie looked at Bolan uneasily, looked at the two youngsters who were watching the conversation in fascination.

"I'll talk to you later," Hanchovini growled. He stomped out of the house, forgetting to complete whatever errand had brought him there in the first place.

"Shit," Edgar Twichen breathed, "I never saw anyone talk to Mr. Hanchovini like that."

Melody Megrims said nothing. She held herself straighter and methodically spooned soup into her mouth. There was anger in every movement.

Bolan sighed. He didn't want to lose the empathy that had been slowly building between himself and this young prostitute. Bolan had always lived close to the line, close to extinction, and he was never closer to meeting death than he was at this moment with the bullets festering in his shoulder and fever racking his body. There was no room in Bolan's life for self-deception. He knew why this young woman mattered to him. He knew it all too well. And he thought of his kid sister, Cindy, who had been pressed into service as a hooker for the Mafia.

Bolan shook off the thought and looked up from his empty soup bowl at the young woman who mechanically fed herself, holding in her contempt now that he had admitted belonging to the Mob. Intuitively Bolan knew her story. It was a story that had been branded on his brain.

"What are you going to do about your wounded shoulder?" Twichen asked.

"I'll decide after I've talked to Johnny Gray," Bolan answered.

"Johnny Gray a friend of yours?"

"You might say that."

"I told you he won't be back from the studio until this evening. He's waiting for Patricia."

"Who's Patricia?" Bolan asked.

Twichen smiled and shrugged to show that he knew he was being pumped and didn't care. He answered, "Patricia Dane is one of the actresses at Lion's Gate Productions. She's really very talented."

Melody Megrims gave a derisive snort.

"Well, you couldn't do it!" Twichen flared at her.

"Frigging right I couldn't do it," Megrims said. "That doesn't mean it takes talent."

"You're just jealous because she gets big money earning an honest living and you're just a hooker."

Bolan had finished eating the nourishing soup and several slices of bread. He leaned back against the wall, too exhausted to interfere in an argument between the porn actor and the prostitute. But he kept his ears open. Everything he could learn increased his almost nonexistent odds of survival. He had bought a little time by bluffing Frankie Hanky, but it would not take long for the Mafia to find out that no one knew someone called C.C.

"You're just jealous of the money she makes," Twichen muttered.

"Enough," Bolan said. His voice was weary.

"She doesn't earn that much. She's always broke," Twichen protested.

Bolan leaned forward and grabbed Megrims's arm. It was clean.

She pulled her arm away. "Do you want to see my thighs, too?"

Bolan shook his head. "I know you're clean. I just wondered if it was ever any other way."

"It never was any other way, Mr. Hotshot Mobster."

Bolan turned to Twichen. "The reason she's always broke is the Mob takes everything she makes to pay off the vigorish on a loan."

"How do you know?" Twichen demanded.

"I've seen it happen before." Bolan's voice was soft, sad.

"Only a fool takes money from a shark," Twichen said self-righteously.

"Only a fool gets involved with the Mob," Bolan told him.

Bolan's mind was not fully on what he was saying. He could not blame it all on the fever, either. He had broken his role camouflage for many reasons, but they all boiled down to a young lady called Melody Megrims, a young lady so much like his sister.

He was tempted to ask Megrims what it was like, to try and get a detailed picture of what his sister had gone through in those last days when he wasn't there to comfort her, to talk to her. But he didn't ask. He could imagine, but that didn't matter, either.

Bolan shifted his gaze to the handsome young man.

Twichen had managed to preserve his ideal by compart-mentalizing his mind. Even he didn't deserve the hell that he'd face when reality smashed those compartments. Bolan wondered if he could get through the smug self-satisfaction of the youth, to encourage him to get out before it was too late.

Bolan knew his life hung by a very thin thread. Infection was eating at his shoulder, fever was eating at his body. Without medical help he did not have long, and he had little strength. But what strength he had, had to be used to pull his brother and these two out of the morass of evil that was sucking them under.

Bolan looked around the room, the projection screen painted on the far wall, the mattresses all over the floor. He recognized the pattern.

"So this is where the young ones get introduced," Bolan said.

Twichen smirked. "Yeah, they come in with their dates. Boy, do they get turned on by some of the movies we make."

"And the mattresses are already there," Bolan finished for him. "Who takes the pictures?"

"There's strobes in the ceiling," Twichen explained. "The kids think they're disco lights. We got recruiters in all the schools. They bring the kids in and take pictures by the strobe flashes. They work out real good.

"Then the photographs are used to blackmail the kids into making more blue movies to recruit more kids," Bolan said, unable to keep the disgust out of his voice.

Melody Megrims's voice was strangely gentle when she answered him, "Not even the Mob needs that many untalented actresses. Most of them are given drugs and then forced into prostitution. It doesn't take long to turn them into full-time hookers to pay for their habit."

Megrims suddenly switched the subject. "You're not Mob, are you?"

Bolan fought back a wave of shudders that went through his body before answering, "What makes you think that?"

"You're sick. You have a fever. You're not sharp, whoever you are. You can't keep the disgust off your face. You're not Mob."

Bolan took several deep breaths and looked into those blue eyes across from him. They'd lost most of their dullness. He found a burning intensity there. He knew he had to risk everything to save this woman. She was worth saving.

"I'm not Mob," he admitted.

"So what happens when Mr. Hanchovini checks out your story?" Twichen demanded.

"He may not check, but there'll have to be a showdown sooner or later."

Twichen sneered. "You're not in shape for a showdown with a two-year-old."

"Do you like the part your pictures play in what they do to these kids?" Bolan asked.

"Sex never hurt anybody!" Twichen's voice was loud, showing he felt himself under attack.

"And the drugs? And the blackmail?"

Twichen jumped to his feet, screaming, "I don't have to take this. Especially from a loser!" He ran from the room.

"Why did you tell him you weren't Mafia?" Megrims demanded. "You've just thrown your life away."

Bolan felt very tired. "I'm sick," he told her. "I'm not too sick to fight the jackals, but I'm too sick, too tired, to lie."

"There's more to it than that," Melody Megrims whispered.

"You don't lie to friends," Bolan told her. "It's as simple as that."

"Even if the truth kills you?"

"Even if the truth kills me."

4

Melody Megrims stood over Bolan and offered him her hands.

"Time to move," she told him.

Bolan simply looked at her.

"Hurry," she urged. "I can hide you in my room for a little while, but you have to get up there without being seen. If people start coming in and out, I won't be able to get you tucked away before Eddy comes back with the Mob."

"What makes you think he'll do that?"

"Eddy would make the perfect bureaucrat. His first concern will be to cover his own ass."

"Strange instinct for a porn actor," Bolan muttered.

"You know what I mean. Come on!"

Bolan still made no attempt to move. His fevered eyes were fixed on Megrims's blue ones. The dullness had vanished and there was a sparkle in her eyes for the first time since he'd arrived.

"You don't talk like a prostitute," Bolan said.

"I'm a prostitute so how I talk is like a whore. If you really want to know, the loan that got me into this was to finish my M.A. in social work. I try to cover that up, but in times of stress my education shows through. Now let's go."

Bolan put out his good arm and she tugged, helping him to his feet. He staggered once and then leaned against the wall. He was suddenly unsure of his ability to walk.

"Come on," Megrims urged. "We don't have all day."

Bolan was gathering his energy to take a step on the shifting mattresses, when he heard the front door opening. A few seconds later, a skinny, tired-looking redhead poked her head in the door and said in a cheerful voice, "Hi, Melody." She paused and looked Bolan up and down carefully, then asked, "Who's your good-looking, but well-used friend?"

"Hi, Zenia. I'll introduce you, if you bring a chair," Megrims countered.

"The floor's good and soft."

"My friend's too stiff to get up and down easily."

"Stiff's the way we like them," the redhead said as she disappeared.

In a moment, she returned with a wooden kitchen chair, which she put on the patch of bare floor near the projector. Bolan staggered over and collapsed into it.

"What's wrong with him?" Zenia wanted to know.

"Zenia, this is Corsaro, better known as C.C."

"C.C., Zenia's in the same trade I am, but she's pregnant so she has it soft."

"Soft's no fun," Zenia said in a sad voice.

"She likes her work," Melody explained to Bolan. "There are very few like her."

The redhead laughed. "Don't make me sound like a freak. I won't be working for another three months, anyway."

Melody explained, "Used to be when one of us hookers got pregnant, it was wham-bam through an abortion on the kitchen table and back to work in two or three days. But these days the Mob finds there's more money in looking after us."

Zenia shuddered at Melody's description. "I think it's a real service. There's lots of people who want kids and can't have them. So what's wrong with what we do?"

Bolan knew what was wrong with what they did. He hadn't realized the Mafia had gotten its filthy hands into the illegal adoption business. The idea turned his stomach.

The young prostitutes got pregnant, the Mafia looked after them and when the child came, it was sold. They'd probably get ten or twenty thousand for a healthy child. It might possibly be from people who were unsuitable and couldn't get a child through regular adoption agencies. Some child condemned to a miserable, warped upbringing, so the Mafia could put more money in their rotten coffers.

"Is it a real service to the child?" Bolan asked.

The young prostitute shrugged. "I guess it's better than getting flushed down the crapper."

Bolan felt old. He felt tired. He had no answer, no argument.

"I'll be late for my appointment at the beauty parlor," Zenia said. She was already heading for the door. She left the house two minutes after she had entered.

"Now we've got to get you up the stairs before Eddy comes back with some of the Mob. It's two floors and—" Melody began.

She was interrupted by the sound of the front door opening.

"I wonder what Zenia forgot?" Melody said. She turned to face the doorway but it wasn't the redhead.

The man in the doorway did not look particularly forebidding, merely revolting. But Bolan knew differently. The man stood five foot nine and weighed 150 pounds. His long, black hair was pulled back into a ponytail, revealing a red scar that ran from his left ear to the center of his throat, a souvenir from a victim who did not like his collection methods.

Bolan had no trouble putting a name to this mobster. He was another of Schizzetto's lieutenants from his California days: Pico "The Picker" Pellico, a vulture who preyed on innocents.

Pico's specialty was hanging around colleges and high schools, where he loaned money and peddled drugs. He didn't care how he got the kids hooked, as long as he got them well hooked. Once in The Picker's clutches, young people had only one way to go. Prostitution for the women, theft or prostitution for the boys.

Bolan knew now how Melody Megrims had been hooked by the mob. The Picker was the loan shark who had introduced her to debt, whose interest rates of two or three thousand percent made it impossible to repay. And now that she was a highly paid prostitute, those same interest rates would make it impossible for her ever to pay off her debt, impossible for her ever to get off the path that led straight to hell. Correct that, Bolan thought, that path *is* hell.

"You don't look ready for work," Pico told Melody.

Bolan had only to glance at the young woman to see how terrified she was of Pico Pellico. Pico was much admired by his brothers in corruption. It was said he could work on a girl for a whole hour and send her out on the street without a bruise showing. None of the Mob gave a damn about the bruises on the soul.

Before Melody could say something to compromise either of them, Bolan spoke. "Hello, Picker."

The dark, scarred face studied Bolan intently. "Who the hell are you?"

Bolan grinned, trying to mask the pain he knew must be showing on his face. "You know, that's the second time I've been asked that today? I'll give you the same answer I gave Frankie Hanky. I'm C.C., Corsaro Cancellari. Mr. Cancellari to you. And before you ask me what I'm doing here, I'll also give you the message that I told Hanky to deliver to the Little Squirt. If you don't already know, check with New York."

The sureness and the aggressiveness in Bolan's tone unnerved The Picker. "I'm...I'm sorry...Mr. Cancellari. I don't know New York. No offense. I just came to get my payment from this slut."

Bolan turned to Melody. "Take a walk, but be around when I call. This gentleman and I have some business to talk. You read?"

Melody looked at Bolan in surprise, then shrugged her shoulders and walked out of the room.

Bolan waited until she was out of earshot, then said to Pellico, "I've got orders concerning you, Pico."

The hood looked down at Bolan, who was still seated in the chair. "What orders?" Orders from the "head shed" made mobsters nervous. Pellico was no exception.

"First, you tell me something."

The Picker sniffed suspiciously. "Like what?"

"Like my shoulder, Pico. Did you send the man who put two bullets in it?"

"Why in hell would I do that?"

Bolan's voice suddenly became cold, remorseless. "I asked you nice. You want me to tell New York that when I came to Canada to straighten this mess up, someone put two bullets in me and you wouldn't give me a straight answer about who did it?"

"I don't know what the hell you're talking about."

Bolan knew that Pico didn't know what he was talking about. The bullets in Bolan's shoulder came from an agent of the DGI—The Dirección General de Inteligencia—but

Bolan would use the situation as a wedge to separate Pellico from his don.

"I'll lay it out for you simply," Bolan snarled. "Certain people are very unhappy about what's happening here. I've been sent to straighten the mess out. I had to pick up a mess after Little Squirt in Frisco and it looks as if I'll have to pick up after him here."

"What mess? I don't know what you're talking about."

Bolan lowered his voice to a confidential monotone. "Listen, Pico, you're an expert in what you do. We haven't missed that in New York. The trouble is you haven't been given enough reponsibility or this mess would have never happened, right?"

"Yeah, I know what I'm doing but—"

"But nothing. You're the best talent scout we've got. On top of that you're looking after all the enforcement in the area, aren't you?"

In spite of himself, Pellico was impressed that New York was aware of his services. He was confused, off balance and not a little flattered.

"Well, yeah," The Picker said, gaining confidence.

"The Squirt got too big for his britches in Frisco. He thought no one could touch him so he went after a couple of starlets. Now we pick up the papers and it sounds like his britches are too damn tight again. His prostitutes can't walk the street without being harassed. The outlets for his video tapes get fire-bombed—"

"Hell, that was a bunch of terrorist nuts."

"I don't give a damn who it was," Bolan snapped. "There's no profit in getting our product fire-bombed. It makes others reluctant to handle it. The women don't make money while their johns are being harassed. You get that?" Bolan winced.

"I guess so."

"Don't guess. Know! And all this labor unrest. How big a muscle squad have you put together to back the strikers?"

"Back the strikers! They're going to lose."

"Have we got a handle on the unions here, Pico?"

"Nah, we don't get an edge on most of these damn B.C. unions."

"So when the government sets them up, makes them ready to be thankful to the first help they get, Schizzetto doesn't tell you to get ready and give them some of that help—so we can move in?"

Standing in front of Bolan's chair, the Mafia goon shifted uncomfortably. "Well, no. I haven't..."

"You should have! He's getting too big for his britches again. Did he tell you to send the bastard who winged me?"

The Picker was distinctly uncomfortable and he was beginning to sweat. "Nah. No one told me to."

"Relax, Picker. I believe you. What guns has Squirt got that don't come through you?"

"Only his house man. That's ail."

"So when I look over the Squirt's guard, I'll find the son of a bitch," Bolan told the enforcer. Waves of darkness were crashing on the shores of his consciousness. He was beginning to wonder how long he could keep this up.

"Look, there must be some mistake."

"No mistake on your part, Picker. But a big mistake on someone's. I've got special orders about you. If you're clean, you're to be left to grow best you can. You haven't been given enough responsibility. You'll get it soon."

The Picker looked suspiciously at Bolan. "So what do you want me to to do?"

"Loyalty's a good thing, Picker. No man should have to go back on his loyalty."

Picker nodded doubtfully.

"So all you have to do is keep your nose clean and your mouth shut, savvy? I'll tell the Little Squirt what's happening to him. I'll deliver the commission's message, when the time comes. In the meantime, you play business as usual. Got it?"

"And I'm clean?" Pellico was obviously having difficulty convincing himself of his good fortune. The immense pressure suddenly lifted when he found that none of the blame was being attached to him. His immediate feeling was one of gratitude; it showed on his face.

"Hey, I'm not asking you to betray anyone. I'm just asking you to look after your own best interests. Start moving ahead."

"Sure, C.C. Anything you say. Thanks. Is there anything I can do? What about your shoulder?"

"Don't worry about my shoulder. Just don't give the game away and you'll come out way ahead. And, ah...there is one small thing."

Pellico was only too anxious to supply whatever this enforcer from the head shed wanted.

"The girl. The one who was in here. Can she stay with me for a few days? I gotta admit it, Picker, you sure can pick them."

"Sure, C.C. Be glad to. I'll tell her."

"I'm not going to move for a few days. I've got things to investigate. I won't take her if it's going to give the game away," Bolan told the procurer.

"Don't worry, C.C. I'll take care of everything."

"Thanks, Pico. New York told me I could count on you."

Pellico left the room glowing. He found Melody in the kitchen of the Mafia youth trap.

"You listen to me and listen good," Picker growled at Megrims. "That C.C., you take care of him. If he complains about you, I'll tear both your tits off. You got that?"

Megrims was so stunned she could only nod.

"Get in there now and stay with him. You don't do anything else, or look after anyone else till you're told different. Now get."

Having given his orders, the Picker turned on his heel and left the house, whistling.

Melody went back into the front room with its solid mattress furniture, folded her arms and stared at Bolan.

"Are you Mob or aren't you?" she asked.

"If you have to ask, no answer I can give will convince you."

She thought about that for a few seconds. "What did you tell Mr. Pellico?"

"That I'm here on Mafia business and I'd consider it a courtesy if he'd give you to me while I'm here."

"And you convinced him?"

"So it seems."

"And you convinced me that you weren't Mafia."

Bolan was rapidly running out of energy and found it hard to focus on the conversation. Her doubts were genuine, but they were her doubts. He could do nothing to help her solve those.

"I didn't convince you of anything," he told her. "You made that decision for yourself. The question isn't how much you trust me; it's how much you trust your own judgment."

Melody thought about it for a few more seconds, before deciding, "Now you're going to have both Hanchovini and Pellico looking for your ass when they find they've been taken. I'd better get you out of sight damned fast. Let's go."

Bolan gave her a weak smile and started to get up, but collapsed in the chair.

"I can't make it?" he asked.

"You've got to! If Edgar comes back with someone, we're both dead. You've got to move!"

Bolan knew she was right. He drew on the last of his failing strength and staggered to his feet. She grabbed his arm to keep him from falling and led him toward the door.

"Hurry," she breathed. "Someone may come at any moment."

The stairs were a nightmare, two flights of them. By the first landing, Bolan was out of breath. His head swam.

The second flight of stairs Bolan tackled on hands and knees. Melody alternately pulled on his good arm and pushed him from behind, keeping him moving, grunting, not letting him stop. The hall and stairs no longer swayed from side to side like the deck of a ship in a storm. They narrowed. There was blackness outside. There was only the step in front of him, only the small amount of bare hall in front of his nose; all the rest was blackness.

Bolan was still moving. He was on his stomach. Crawling. His senses no longer kept him informed, but he could hear Melody Megrims running commentary. Its urgency escaped him. He continued to move inch by inch, holding onto life and consciousness with nothing but grim determination. Her voice was merely a background sound. He understood the words, but they didn't seem to apply to him.

"My God, it's the door! I hear Edgar's voice. He has someone with him. It's only fifteen more feet. Move faster! They're coming up the stairs. Hurry."

But Bolan couldn't move. His arms and legs stopped working. He lay there drenched in his own perspiration and shivering. He was conscious, aware, but the stairs had taken the last of his reserves. He could go no farther.

5

Johnny Bolan Gray held open the front door of Lion's Gate Productions Ltd., allowing Patricia Dane to step out into the street first. Dane immediately attracted several stares from pedestrians. Not all the glances were friendly. She certainly stood out in a crowd, despite her small stature.

Dane wore spike heels, and net stockings that barely had room to disappear under a short black leather skirt. Her sweater was woven loosely from string, the weave sufficiently open to show that she had nothing on underneath. Her breasts were small, firm mounds that needed no support. Chestnut hair fell down her back to her waist. Her makeup was garish, excessive, but it served its purpose. It made her look about nineteen. Without it she would have looked twelve or thirteen.

Johnny was dressed in jeans and a navy-blue T-shirt. His dark hair, unruly at the best of times, was in need of a trim and almost covered his ears. He wore glasses with light plastic frames.

Their progress along the sidewalk was suddenly impeded by a half-dozen women dressed in expensive, but dowdy clothing. One of them, a woman in her forties, wearing a baggy gray pants suit, pointed at Johnny and yelled, "Shame on you, john. Shame on you with a prostitute."

The rest of the group, four other women and one hen-pecked man, all pointed at Johnny and started yelling, "Shame on you, john."

"They think I'm a prostitute!" Dane said. Her voice quivered with indignation.

"I wonder what could have given them that idea," Johnny said mildly.

"Don't start that again," Dane said. "An actress has to dress with some flare. I like the way I dress."

Johnny felt it was an inopportune time to argue with the girl about the way she dressed. However, it was the main reason he had gone to the studio and waited to walk her home. Dressed this way, she was no longer safe on Vancouver streets.

At first the Vancouver citizens had been content merely to harass the men who stopped to talk to the prostitutes. Soon they were harassing the whores themselves. Two hookers had been beaten severely by vigilantes a week before. Groups like that judged the women solely on how they dressed.

Johnny knew that Dane was asking for trouble, but she couldn't see his point. He would have sidled around the group or gone across the street, but Dane was affronted. She stopped in front of the ringleader.

"Lady," Dane said in a voice that carried above the shouting of the group, "please don't hassle me. I've been servicing your husband all afternoon. I'm pooped."

Before the group could recover from Dane's outrageous statement, Johnny took her by the elbow and said, "Come on, sis, Mom's going to give you hell when she hears you've been talking like that."

"This girl your sister?" one of the women asked.

"I'm just taking her home from acting class," Johnny said with a straight face.

"Acting class!" Dane exploded.

Johnny's hand suddenly tightened painfully on her upper arm and she bit off whatever else she was going to say. The Vancouver citizens parted to let them pass, but the woman in the pants suit said, "She dresses like a slut."

Dane turned toward her and, in spite of the increasing pressure on her arm, said, "And you dress like a bag lady. Hello, bag lady."

Johnny practically dragged Dane away from the confrontation. He wasn't a particular fan of the self-righteous prigs of Vancouver, but he was more concerned with getting Dane off the street in one piece. She pulled her arm from his grasp.

"The old bag," Dane complained. "How could she have possibly mistaken me for a prostitute!"

"It's the way you dress."

"I have the right to dress any way I want."

"Sure," Johnny told her. "But it may get you beaten within an inch of your life."

Dane ignored Johnny's logic. "I am not a prostitute, I'm an actress. I'll damn well dress the way an actress should dress."

Johnny sighed. They'd been over this ground before. Patricia Dane's problem wasn't that she was a mental lightweight; it was that she was so desperate to be famous, to be known as an actress, that she didn't think straight on the subject.

When Patricia Dane had disappeared from her home in San Diego, her family did not have to be told she would be somewhere where movies were being made; they simply hadn't guessed what kind of movies, nor had they any idea where.

The Danes were still having difficulty coming to terms with the idea of dating without chaperones. That their daughter might be on her way to becoming a porn queen simply never occurred to them.

On the advice of some of his church members, Gunther Dane went to the criminal lawyer Armand Killinger. Killinger would be sympathetic and could be trusted. A young investigator worked for him who could move in among Patricia's friends and find out what had happened to her.

That was how Johnny Bolan Gray found himself taking temporary leave from his legal-aid service to undertake a full-time investigation for Armand. Usually he split his time between working for Killinger and the Free Legal Aid Center.

At first, it had seemed the investigation would be only for a couple of days. But it did not take Johnny long to discover that Patricia Dane had fallen in with the wrong kind of movie producer. Neither Johnny nor Killinger wanted to break the news to Dane that his daughter had gone to Canada to make blue movies. So they merely reported that the investigation was continuing and Johnny took off to Vancouver to find the errant daughter and try to persuade her to go home.

He had found her living in a house used for luring teenagers into debt, pornography, prostitution, drugs, and into hell itself. The problem was compounded by the fact that in the eyes of the British Columbia government, at nineteen Patricia Dane was legally an adult. She could not be forced to return to her parents.

Johnny did the only thing he knew to do. He made himself a part of the group of young people who lived in the house where Dane stayed on Jackson Street, keeping his eye on Dane and doing what he could to influence her.

He let Armand Killinger know where he was, leaving Armand to deal with the distraught family. Then he put an urgent message into underground channels. Actually several urgent messages, hoping one of them would reach Mack, hoping his brother would come and deal with the stinking Mafia mess Johnny had found in Vancouver.

Patricia Dane had sunk into the foulest morass known to man. She was submerged up to her beautiful neck in the corruption of the Mafia and still did not realize that she was in danger. All Johnny could do was keep an eye on her and hope that Mack would arrive in time to drain this particular, polluted swamp.

Johnny walked beside Dane, worried because he had not yet heard from his brother. It had been hopeless to try and talk Patricia Dane out of her present course. To her, making pornographic films was just a step toward stardom.

The Mafia had done a smooth job of convincing her that once she was seen on the blue screen, Hollywood producers would be anxious to have her acting in legitimate films. It was not as difficult a selling job as Johnny might have imagined. Hanchovini merely had to point at the amount of nudity and sex in the Hollywood films as proof that a blue movie was the best stepping stone to the top.

"Let's have a beer," Dane said as she and Johnny entered the house on Jackson Street.

"Suits me," Johnny replied. He followed her down the hall, toward the kitchen in the back of the main floor.

Dane entered the kitchen a few steps ahead of Johnny. She found Twichen draining one beer bottle and holding another open one in his hand.

"Leave some for us, Eddy," she told him.

Twichen paid no attention to Dane's words. Instead, he started saying what was on his mind, despite the fact that there was no context, no way Dane could make sense of what he was saying. "I'm the one who brought that damn doctor. But do they have any thanks. No. 'It's out of the way, Eddy.' 'You're in the way, 'Eddy.' 'We've got to operate, Eddy.' Hell, I probably saved...'' Twichen abruptly cut off his monologue of self-pity when Johnny entered the kitchen. ''What the hell are you doing here?''

Johnny had heard enough of Twichen's monologue to know that the anger was not really directed at him. He smiled and told the porn actor, ''Thanks, Eddy. I will have a beer.''

''No one invited you.''

''I invited him.'' Dane said. ''I'll get the beer.''

She pushed past the surprised Twichen and took two more bottles out of the refrigerator. She opened them and handed one to Johnny.

As the three of them settled into kitchen chairs, Dane asked, ''What were you complaining about, Eddy?''

Twichen cast a sly glance at Johnny Bolan and clamped his mouth shut. Then after he'd thought about it for a few seconds he answered Dane, ''Just frothing at the mouth. Don't pay any attention to me.''

''That's easy,'' she said.''

''So it seems,'' Twichen replied. His voice was bitter. ''You've got no time for your leading man, but you can waste your time with this bum.''

''Don't be jealous. Johnny was at the studio to see what it's like. You know Mr. Hanchovini would like him to try for a part. If you'd been there to meet me after work, I'd have come home with you.'' She paused and glanced at Johnny. ''You're all right, Johnny, but you're still trying to mother me. At least Eddy doesn't object to the way I dress. Do you, Eddy?''

''As long as I can figure how to take it off, wear what you like.'' Eddy paused to roll his eyes.

Johnny had no intention of competing for Dane. First, he wasn't all that interested. But more important, when he advised her to get out and get away from the Mafia, he could hardly afford to be accused of sounding like a jealous lover. He took a swig of beer and set the bottle down more noisily than necessary.

"Don't let me get in your way. I'll be on my way as soon as I finish this beer," Johnny told them.

As soon as the words were out, Johnny could see he'd made another tactical error. Patricia Dane wanted the attention of two men. She'd be delighted if they'd actually do physical battle over her. Her attitude did nothing to make her more attractive to Johnny.

"Do hang around, Johnny. I'm sure we can find something interesting to do," Dane said.

Johnny was aware that Dane was making a play for him in order to pit him against Twichen. Having already decided not to be suckered into that trap, he stood up and pushed back his chair, leaving the unfinished beer on the kitchen table. But before he could say anything else, the front door opened and Hanchovini's voice drifted down the hall.

"Heard someone in the kitchen. Let's look there first."

No one in the kitchen spoke as they listened to the sound of Frankie Hanky's heavy tread followed by the lighter, faster footsteps of a smaller man. Frankie, in his usual gray suit, stepped into the kitchen. He was followed by a short, bald man of about fifty. The man was wearing tailored slacks, a silk shirt open at the neck and Gucci loafers. A long straight nose accented the features of a weasel.

"Where is he?" Frankie Hanky asked.

Johnny Bolan deliberately chose to have his reaction contrast with that of Twichen and Dane, who glanced at each other nervously and said nothing.

"I'm here. What more do you want?" Johnny said.

The two predators didn't see any joke. Humor, to them, had to be based on sex or suffering. Not knowing how to deal with Johnny's remark, they ignored it.

Frankie Hanky turned to Twichen, who was the only one of the trio who had been there when he had met C.C. "C.C., Cancellari, where is he?"

Twichen took too long drinking his beer before answering. Johnny surmised that he was getting his face in order, to cover up guilty knowledge. When Twichen put down the bottle, he said, "How should I know? He left shortly after you did. Want a beer?"

Johnny was not the only one to notice Twichen's unusual behavior. Dane tried to give him time to recover by asking, "Who are you talking about?"

"Corsaro Cancellari, C.C. What business is it of yours?" Frankie Hanky demanded in an icy voice.

"He was wounded," Twichen explained. "He must have gone somewhere to get patched up."

The words stabbed Johnny. The name was too good to be true. Johnny hoped that it was a message for him. Corsaro Cancellari was Italian for "I cancel pirates." Both were legitimate Italian names, but together it was too much of a coincidence.

Frankie Hanky grabbed Twichen's hair and yanked him out of his chair. Then the Mafia king's open palm stung the porn actor's cheek twice.

"Enough of this shit. Where the hell's Cancellari?"

"I don't know. Honest. Ask Johnny. He came here looking for Johnny Gray."

Twichen sank back into his chair and tried to make himself look insignificant. Both Mafia hoods turned toward Johnny.

6

Johnny stood up straighter, not allowing his despair to show. Mack was here—great! But he was wounded. Johnny's gut knotted. Armand Killinger had told Johnny more than once, "The only lawyer who survives trial work is the one who can think on his feet. You can't afford to show surprise, not on your face, nor in the way you stand, nor by hesitating. If you can't get that right, you don't belong in trial work."

Johnny had worked hard at getting that right. The training paid off in that one moment.

"I didn't know C.C. was wounded. What happened?" Johnny demanded. His voice acquired a sudden ring of hard authority.

The two hoods were accustomed to the young people cringing. Johnny's calm hard voice made them stop and glance at each other.

"What do you know about this Cancellari shit?" Frankie demanded.

"I know that if he finds out you called him a shit, you're a dead man. Now what the hell's this about him being wounded?"

When Frankie Hanky found that Johnny was not going to be intimidated, he paused again. Frankie and the other hood were within two feet of Johnny. After a moment's consideration, Frankie Hanky decided to answer Johnny's question, to see where the information would lead.

"He says he got shot when he came here to investigate. Seems like he took two in the shoulder. Now if you don't tell me what you know about this guy, I'm going to break your neck."

Johnny faced down Frankie with a calmness he did not feel. "Don't get tough with me, Hanchovini."

The mobster had to think about that for a couple of seconds. "Do you work for Cancellari?"

"I was to come ahead and have a report for him."

Hanchovini's voice grew soft, dangerous. "Then perhaps you can explain how come C.C. says he cleaned up a mess after the boss in Frisco?"

"If C.C. says he cleaned up the mess, he cleaned up the mess."

The small, weasel-like hood spoke for the first time. His voice was high and squeaky, adding to the image of a rodent. "I was a member of Roman's family at that time. I didn't know no damn C.C."

Johnny found what thinking on his feet was like. He'd identified himself with C.C. Now he had to come out on top in this battle of wits or there was a good chance both he and Mack would go down together.

"Did he say he was in the DeMarco family?" Johnny demanded in a firm voice.

"He said he'd cleaned up a mess there," Frankie reiterated.

"I didn't work for him then, but I'm pretty sure I know who he was working for at that time, and it wasn't the west coast.

Frankie Hanky took the comment the way Johnny intended him to. "Hell. He's from the New York head shed."

Johnny was not going to be lured into making statements that would contradict Mack's story. "I didn't say that," he snapped.

"Are you saying that he isn't?"

"I'm not saying that, either."

Frankie Hanky nodded as if he'd had all the proof he needed that his hunch was correct. "What the hell's he doing here?"

"Even if I knew, I wouldn't answer questions about the boss's business. You ask him." Johnny's voice was cold enough to make Patricia Dane shiver.

"You better come with me until we get this thing straightened out," Hanchovini decided.

"If that's the way you want to stand with C.C., let's go."

"Hey, come off it, Johnny. I treated you all right, even though you were lying to me about who you are, spying on me. I'm just asking you nice to come along and talk to my boss."

"And my orders are to stay here until C.C. tells me otherwise."

"Then C.C.'s going to come back here for you?" Frankie Hanky asked.

"Either that or show up at my place," Johnny answered. Johnny had taken a room near the Mafia house. No one had invited him to move in. Johnny was not sure he would have, even if it had been offered. His job was to get Patricia Dane out, not to get tangled with the Mob.

"And he's New York, works for the head shed."

"That's for him to answer," Johnny replied.

"As soon as you see your boss, tell him it's time for him to pay his official respects. You got it?"

"I got it," Johnny answered. He put respect into his voice to mollify the mobster for the lack of information.

The two hoods nodded, turned on their heels, and left without saying anything else.

As soon as they were out the door, Patricia Dane demanded, "If you're a member of the Mob, how come you're so all fired up to get me to leave this place?"

Johnny had no answer. His story would not hold up under the day-to-day scrutiny of these young people. On the other hand, if he admitted not being Mafia, he'd place the lives of both himself and Mack in the hands of these two spoiled brats. He decided to ignore the question and have some of his own answered instead. He grabbed Twichen by the shirtfront and hauled him out of his chair.

"Where the hell's C.C.?"

Twichen was unsure what was happening. The man upstairs had said he was not Mob. Johnny Gray had convinced the mob that C.C. was a mobster. It was getting too complicated for Twichen's one-track mind.

"Let go of me," he demanded.

"You won't look too good under a camera if I don't get an answer, now."

"He says he isn't Mob. Is he?"

Again it was a question Johnny couldn't answer. He sank his fist into Twichen's stomach, causing him to double up and fall back into the chair. It took him several minutes of painful gasping to get his diaphragm working again.

"He's…he's up in Melody's room. I even got a doctor for him. And this is all the thanks I get."

"Thanks," Johnny said in a flat voice. He'd already turned on his heel and was headed for the stairs.

Dane looked at Twichen, who was still holding his stomach in agony. "Is Johnny really Mafia?"

"The bastard. I'll kill him for this," Twichen gasped.

Dane smiled. "I doubt it. I also doubt Johnny has anything to do with the Mob. If they find out this is a bluff, they'll work him over something fierce."

"After what I did for his friend, he damn near kills me. I hope they kill him," Twichen gasped.

"If they're really faking it, it would make great information for Mr. Hanchovini," Dane mused. "I'll bet he could even get me a part in a Hollywood film."

"Don't play around with them," Twichen warned. "One way or the other, you end up getting hurt."

"You're right. We should stay out of it," Dane told him. She was smiling.

WHEN DR. ELEONORA VOLTA turned over the body on the floor of Melody Megrims's room, she knew she was looking at a dead man.

She laid the body flat on its back and placed a fingertip on the temple. There was a pulse, much too rapid. The head was hot, the breathing shallow and fast. She stopped and looked at the face for a long time. The fingers gently probed the short sideburns. Knowing what to look for, she found the traces of more than one face-change operation.

The eyes blinked open for a few seconds and worked to focus on Dr. Volta's face. A faint flicker of a smile passed over the mouth, then the patient slipped back into unconsciousness. Nothing could change those eyes.

"Dr. Volta, are you all right?" There was concern in Melody Megrims's voice as she addressed the only doctor in Vancouver who would treat a shooting victim without calling the police. As Dr. Volta saw it, if it weren't for her, an injured gangster might die rather than seek help, if it meant the police would be notified. And Volta's main interest was in saving lives—even the lives of mobsters and desperate men like the one before her now.

Eleonora Volta shook herself. She forced herself to look at the young prostitute and smile. "I'm all right. Let's see if we can save the life of a dead man. We'll have to move him onto your bed so I can work on him."

"Come on, Eddy. Lend a hand," Megrims told Twichen. It was a struggle, but the three of them managed to move Bolan's inert form onto Megrims's bed. Twichen lifted the good left shoulder while Volta supported the head and did what she could to assist Twichen with the main weight of the body. Megrims handled the legs.

Volta carefully cut away the shirt and lifted the pad of newspaper from the wound. Then she removed her plain gray suit jacket and hung it up. Underneath she wore a severe silk blouse.

Megrims looked at the spotlessly white blouse which must have cost $200, and offered, "Do you want something to put on over your blouse?"

Volta smiled as she said, "No thanks. I don't plan to be sloppy today."

She cleared a bedside table, covered it with a sterile towel and opened her huge medical bag. As she carefully laid out her emergency instruments, she told Melody, "You'll have to help."

Painting Bolan's shoulder with antiseptic, she told Twichen, "Close the door on your way out and see that we aren't disturbed."

"I can help here," Twichen protested.

"Possibly, but I'd rather rely on Miss Megrims. Now, go. I've work to do."

Twichen left sulkily, slamming the door behind him.

Melody cocked a quizzical eyebrow at the slim, black-haired doctor. "What made you decide I'd be a better assistant than Eddy?"

"You will, won't you? Wash your hands and arms with this alcohol, then watch closely how I put these gloves on."

Melody had to be shown how to hold the gloves to keep them sterile. She was a quick study and soon had her own pair on. Then Volta began examining the wound and assessing the damage.

"Looks like two bullets, both of them still in there. They've been there for some time; it's a wonder he's survived. Must have the constitution of a bull elephant," Volta muttered, more to herself than to Melody.

Once she was committed to the operation, Eleonora Volta moved with quickness and precision. She made three-inch incisions along the length of the muscle, one deep cut through each bullet hole. The bullets were quickly removed. It took more time to clean out the dead tissue and leave antibiotics in its place. Thirty minutes after she began, Volta tied the last stitch in Bolan's shoulder.

The surgeon picked up her instruments and towels, loading them into a plastic bag. She was silent, thoughtful, while she worked. When she was finished she sat on a corner of the bed, facing the only chair in the room.

At that moment there was a knock on the door, and before anyone could move, Johnny Bolan Gray came in without waiting to be invited. He took two steps into the room before he realized he had entered with undue haste. He stopped, opened his mouth to apologize, then shut it again. He then turned and went to the bed. He stood looking down at the unconscious form for a long time. When Johnny turned, his body was as rigid as a plank.

"Will he live?" he asked Volta.

"Do you know him?" she countered.

"I was told he was asking for me. I was hoping that he'd live long enough to tell me why."

But Volta had seen the change in Johnny's face. "You know who he really is, don't you?" she said softly.

Johnny looked from Volta to Megrims and then turned to stare at the pale figure on the bloody bed.

"Yes," Johnny Bolan Gray admitted. "He's my brother."

7

"That's a dangerous admission," said Melody Megrims.

"What makes you say that? Isn't Corsaro among friends?"

"That remains to be seen, obviously," said Dr. Volta. "In the meantime, he'll need round-the-clock nursing. You can split the chores with Miss Megrims. It might be wise for you to be around, even when you aren't on nursing duty."

"Thanks for looking after him. I'll be around to keep my eyes open."

"Miss Megrims can reach me, if I'm needed," said Dr. Volta. "Otherwise, I'll look in tomorrow. When he comes to, give him as much fluid as he can take, and whatever food he wants. Try to get him to eat liver. He's full of antibiotics and won't need more until tomorrow.

"One more thing. You'd better go out and buy a bed-pan. He won't be able to sit up for several days. It was a very near thing." Having said her piece, Dr. Volta hurried out without saying goodbye.

"Is there anything I can do?" Johnny said to Megrims.

Megrims paused to think before answering, "You can start by doing some shopping. Have you any money?" When Johnny nodded, she went on, "Get plenty of good substantial soup, and some staples, including liver. I'll cook. We'll see how much we can get into your brother.

"If you have the money, I'd suggest a couple of air mattresses and light sleeping bags. You might as well stay here until Corsaro's better."

"Hey, couldn't I get you into trouble just staying here?"

"I'm in trouble no matter which way the cookie crumbles. Hanchovini threatened me with a beating if I didn't take good care of Corsaro. I'll be in for a lot worse when they discover Corsaro isn't really Mob."

"Who said Corsaro isn't family?" Johnny demanded.

"I said. Now, get the hell out of here and do the shopping. And don't forget the bedpan and bottle. I sure as hell don't want to have to change my mattress because of you and your brother."

Johnny went to the door, then turned and said with a straight face, "Yes, ma'am."

When the door was closed, Megrim smiled. She stood staring at the closed door for some time before turning and starting to tidy and rearrange the room. Frequently, she glanced at the figure that lay so still in her bed.

It would not be easy putting up with Corsaro and his brother for a couple of weeks. How had she ever gotten involved in this mess? It could end up costing her her life.

She went around the room, picking up her dirty laundry. She used to be neat when she was in college. Now, it no longer seemed to matter. As she stuffed the laundry into a garbage bag, she glanced again at the bed. A pair of blue eyes stared back at her. There were two frown lines between the eyes, as if the owner was trying to figure out where he was and how he came to be there.

Melody tossed the bag of laundry into a corner and sat on the edge of the bed. From close up, his eyes didn't look confused. They seemed to look right through her, to see what she was like inside. She shivered, telling herself she was being silly. She brushed a lock of hair from Corsaro's forehead and rested her hand there. She couldn't be sure, but she thought the fever had already begun to abate.

"You're in my room," Melody told the man she knew as Corsaro Cancellari. "The bullets were removed from your shoulder. You'll get better now. How do you feel?"

Mack Bolan tried to speak several times before he managed to croak the single word "Water."

"Right away," she told him, and hurried down to the kitchen for a clean glass.

It was no easy task to get water into a 200-pound man who could not raise himself from flat on his back. She eventually managed to prop him up with enough pillows and blankets to allow him to drink. If the pulling and shoving hurt the wounded shoulder, he made no outcry or complaint.

He was unable to hold the glass steady. Melody held it for him, giving him a very small amount at a time. The patient was content with small sips, but wanted plenty. It took half an hour to get three glasses of water into him.

In spite of herself, Melody was impressed by the calm, silent way her patient fought to survive. There were no moans, no grimaces, no useless protests. He just kept trying until he had enough water. Melody could not help responding to the tremendous life force which expressed itself through this man.

When the third glass was empty, he relaxed. "Thanks," he breathed.

"Your brother was here. He went out for supplies and should be back soon." The man was oblivious to her news. He made no attempt to speak. In a few seconds, he was unconscious again.

The first short awakening set the pattern for the next two days. Bolan would wake. Johnny or Melody would be there to wash and feed him, give him the bedpan. The patient would then say, "Thanks," and lapse back into unconsciousness. There was no sign he recognized either of them, or could tell one from the other.

Dr. Volta returned twice during that time, to check progress, give shots and change dressings. Each time, her patient would wake, watch what she was doing, whisper, "Thanks," and drift back to sleep.

"He's drawn on more reserves than most human beings have," Volta explained to Johnny. "It will take him a long time to replace his strength. Keep him quiet, keep him fed and let nature do what it can. I'll look in again tomorrow."

However, the next morning Pico "The Picker" Pellico arrived before Volta did. He found Johnny and Melody having a coffee together in the kitchen.

"Where's Cancellari?" Pellico asked Megims.

Melody cast a panicked glance at Johnny.

"I told you to stick with him," Pellico said. "You damn well better know where he is or you're going to hurt so bad you'll have to crawl onto the street."

Johnny started to ease himself out of his chair, ready for trouble. Melody casually placed a restraining hand on his shoulder.

"He's upstairs, in my bed. Where else?" Megrims kept her voice casual.

Pellico turned on his heel to go upstairs.

"Maybe you'd better leave him for another day or two," Melody said, her voice cautious.

Pellico swung back to face her, suspicion written all over his face. "What the hell's going on?"

"He had two bullets taken from his shoulder. He's still pretty weak."

"Why in hell didn't you get him to a hospital? You know we always look after our own."

Megrims stood a little straighter, looking the sadistic pimp in the eye. "It's the way he wanted it. I did as I was told."

"We'll see about that," Pellico snorted. He turned on his heel and strode out of the kitchen and up the stairs.

Johnny brushed off Melody's hand.

"Why'd you tell him where to look?" Johnny demanded.

Melody shrugged and sat down again to her coffee. "Why not? He told me to stay with Corsaro. There's no way I could convince him I don't know where your brother is." She sipped her beverage, refusing to meet Johnny's eyes.

Johnny didn't waste time on words, but silently followed Pellico up the stairs. Pellico had moved swiftly and quietly and Johnny did not catch up until the mobster was in Melody's room.

Before Johnny could do or say anything, Bolan opened his eyes and then grinned at the mobster.

"Morning, Picker. On the early shift?"

Pellico did not answer. He glanced at Johnny, who stood in the doorway, then said, "Just came for a little *private* conversation, Mr. Cancellari."

At the word "private," Bolan glanced at the doorway. Johnny was sure that Mack's eyes widened in surprise as he recognized Johnny for the first time. It was only then that the younger Bolan was certain that his brother would live— if he did not make a slip and give himself away to the mob.

"It's okay, Johnny. The Picker and I are old friends," Mack said. His voice was still weak, but it was much better than the mere whisper he'd been using.

Johnny had no choice but to retreat to the end of the hall. But he was worried about the outcome of the conversation between Pellico and his brother.

The door to Melody's room shut and Johnny heard the mumble of voices from inside but could not make out the words. He had no idea how long Mack could stay alert and keep up his false front. Johnny kept looking at his watch; it seemed to have stopped entirely, but it finally crept around to five minutes from the time the door closed. As soon as the five minutes were up, Johnny walked up the hall, rapped on the door twice, opened it and went in.

Pellico broke off what he was saying in midsentence, glanced up at Johnny and growled, "I didn't hear anyone tell you to come in."

"No one told me to come in, Mr. Pellico. But I must ask you to leave. Corsaro's still weak and the doctor says he's got to take it easy. I don't want any trouble with you, Mr. Pellico, but I'll force you out of here if I have to."

The Picker looked as if he were going to explode, then his scarred face dissolved into a grin.

"Okay, kid. You take good care of him. I'll go." The Picker turned to Bolan. "Don't worry, Corsaro. I'll get the information you want. I'll see you tomorrow or the next day. The way this kid hurries your visitors in and out you should get well soon."

Still chuckling, Pellico left the room, went down the stairs and out of the house.

Bolan looked at his young brother and smiled. "I like the Marines. They land exactly when needed."

"It's good you're feeling better. But you got a lot of resting to do yet..." Johnny did not finish telling Mack how important it was to rest. Mack was already asleep again.

The next morning, Johnny woke to an unfamiliar sound. His eyes flew open and he sat up quickly.

Mack had thrown his covers off and was trying to sit up. Johnny was at his side instantly, easing him back onto the pillow.

"Take it easy. You're still too weak to go dancing."

"Bathroom," Bolan said in a hoarse voice.

"Bathroom nothing! I'll get the bedpan."

Bolan continued to struggle to get up, not wasting energy on argument. Johnny was amazed at how much strength Mack had regained. Johnny could still handle his elder brother easily, but he could sense that it was possible for Mack to make it to the bathroom, if he had an arm to lean on.

"Not today," Johnny said. "I'll help you get there tomorrow."

Bolan gave in and allowed himself to be eased back onto the pillow, but he caught Johnny's arm before he could pull away.

"Tomorrow," Bolan croaked. "Must move on soon. Too long in one place. Dangerous for everyone."

Johnny understood that Mack's compulsion to move was motivated by fear, not for himself, but for those who helped him. Johnny had a brief glimpse at the worst nightmare a man could have—a nightmare that must perpetually ride his brother's back. It was that the animals, whether they were Mafia or terrorists, would come for the helpless, whose only crime was mercy and compassion, and Bolan would find himself too weak to be able to do anything about it.

Johnny searched his mind for something reassuring to say to his brother, something to alleviate some of his fear for the safety of others. No words could hide reality from Mack Bolan, no matter how weak he was.

"We're safer playing the cards we have. If we disappear now, the Mafia will know we've been bluffing," Johnny said.

Bolan thought for a while before answering, "Okay. Bring the bedpan. We'll take one step at a time, but we must talk."

The morning routine went a bit easier that day. Mack was sufficiently conscious to be cooperative instead of merely inert. When Melody gave him his sponge bath, he was more than a little aware of its thoroughness.

"He's definitely feeling better," Melody told Johnny. She turned back to Bolan with a smile. "Relax, my intentions are strictly honorable." She paused to look him up and down and then added, "At least they're honorable while your brother's here."

By the time the patient was cleaned and fed, he dozed off again, but he woke up two hours later and called Melody over to the bed.

"I have to talk to Johnny. Will you warn us if someone's coming?" he asked her.

"Sure," she answered. "I need a shower anyway."

Johnny went over and sat near the bed. He made a point of sitting with his back to Melody, who dressed and undressed as if she still had her room to herself. Johnny, much to Melody's amusement, found this very distracting.

Melody put on a bathrobe, picked up a towel and left the room, saying "I'll be back in half an hour."

"Attractive girl," Bolan remarked.

"You must be feeling better."

"Not you, too," Bolan protested. "Just tell me why we're both here."

Johnny paused to organize his thoughts. He wanted to present them briefly and not tax Mack to the point where he'd doze off while they talked.

Johnny licked his lips, then waded in. He told Mack about tracing Patricia Dane to Canada, about finding she was happy making blue movies, and how he had hollered for help when he found how deeply the Mafia was involved. To Johnny's relief, Mack stayed alert throughout, occasionally asking pointed questions.

"What about the other people at this house?" Bolan asked after Johnny had finished.

"If we can take care of the main menace, they'll probably straighten themselves out."

Bolan shook his head. "Doesn't work that way. If they do nothing to save themselves, you can't do anything for them."

"So what do we do?" Johnny asked.

"We need three things: weapons, information and positive action from Patricia Dane and friends."

"I didn't risk carrying a weapon into Canada," Johnny said. "It's government policy to keep the population unarmed, and I didn't think I was walking into this sort of situation."

He continued. "I put your Beretta under your pillow, but there's only four rounds in the clip. Do you have more weapons or ammunition stashed somewhere else?"

Bolan shook his head.

"Okay. I'll think of something. What about intelligence?"

"I'm already working on that."

"Pellico?"

Bolan nodded.

"What's this about positive action?" Johnny asked.

"These young people have to get themselves out before things start to blow. We can't risk getting them killed. We can't force them to cooperate."

Johnny was still mulling that over when Melody Megrims returned from her shower.

"Enough chitchat," she told Johnny. "Our patient needs his strength."

Johnny was silent for a few seconds. Then he stood up and told his brother, "I won't be back until evening. I know where I can pick up the items we need."

"No!" Bolan said.

But Johnny was already on his way through the door and didn't hear him.

Bolan struggled to sit up. Melody was right there, forcing her damp body against him, pressing him back into the bed. Her hands stroked and soothed his fevered forehead.

8

North Vancouver, considered the most exclusive suburb in the Vancouver area, is peculiar in several ways. On a clear day the view from the mountain is spellbinding, but Mount Seymour is particularly prone to fog. As a result, the more exclusive the location, the less often the inhabitant can enjoy the view.

Rudolfo Schizzetto, the Mafia Don of western Canada, had his estate so far up the mountain that during the foggy season he'd go for weeks without being able to see more than ten feet beyond his windows. It had cost him a million dollars to acquire three acres and have it terraced. By Vancouver standards, his location, high above everyone else, made him the most respectable man in the city.

Johnny Bolan Gray sat in the soggy bush 500 yards up the mountain from the back of Schizzetto's estate, examining the property below with lightweight 8x40 binoculars, planning a soft penetration. It would not be easy. Johnny had no weapon. The three mobsters who patrolled the grounds wore holstered revolvers as part of their security guard uniforms.

The architect had made clever use of the natural terrain to transform an ordinary-looking mansion into a fortress. Like most of the houses in the area, it was obscured from the road by a strip of bush. The bush grew too close to the road for a motorist to see the clearing behind it. However, the house was up four terraced levels and had plenty of clear space in front of it. So the woods did not obstruct the view from the house, of Vancouver and the sea.

A driveway ran through the trees and shrubs to a wrought-iron gate, between two stone posts, part of a wrought-iron fence which surrounded the property. The fence was eight feet high and supported by stone uprights every twenty feet. At the sides and back, the fence was hidden behind a three-foot-thick hawthorne hedge.

Johnny trained the binoculars on the fence. The hedge had been carefully trimmed so that it never actually touched the fence. Johnny considered this adequate proof that the fence was either charged or wired with an alarm system, perhaps both.

Inside the fence, there was little except manicured lawn and the occasional bed of short flowers. The house was two and a half floors of solid brick. The windows were stylish slits, reminiscent of the fortifications designed to protect bowmen in the middle ages. Johnny suddenly had a new appreciation of the term "hardsite."

Johnny knew he lacked his brother's understanding of role camouflage and the weaknesses of the Mafia. Perhaps Mack could do a soft probe, but Johnny was shrewd enough to realize he lacked the experience. So he fell back on the basic tenet of his Marine training: "When in doubt, attack."

He circled the property back to his sky-blue Volkswagen bus, drove to the nearest beer store and bought six cases. The next stop was a convenience store where he bought a thick, black marker. With the marker, he wrote, "Schizzetto" and the address in large letters on each case.

Johnny eased his bus along the curved path through the trees and stopped in front of the wrought-iron gate. In a moment, one of the guards appeared on the other side of the bars. He appeared so quickly Johnny suspected that there were detection devices along the driveway.

"Private property," the mobster yelled, waving for Johnny to go back.

Johnny stuck his head out the window. "Beer delivery for Schizzetto," he called back.

"We ain't expecting no beer."

"You Schizzetto?"

"Hell no! What are you? A smart ass?"

"I'm just a guy trying to make a living delivering beer. I have the right place, don't I?"

"Okay. Give it to me. I'll take it up to the house."

"That's fine with me. Just don't forget to bring back the money and the nine empty cases."

"What the hell are you trying to pull?"

Johnny climbed out of the van, frowning with annoyance. "Take a look for yourself," he told the guard. He threw open the side door of the bus.

The guard opened the gate and came up to the vehicle, keeping one hand near his holster. The sight of the pile of cases of beer, each one bearing the correct name and address, convinced him.

"They're supposed to clear visitors and deliveries with me," the hood complained. "It must be the old man's daughter, throwing another party. She never remembers to let security know."

"Must be a job that needs a lot of diplomacy," Johnny observed as he climbed back behind the steering wheel. It was exactly the right touch. Johnny was the first person ever to sympathize with the gatekeeper.

The hood struggled to hide a grin. "If by diplomacy you mean a guy's wrong no matter what he does, you're right. If I don't enforce the rules, I'm not doing my job. If the beer isn't there for Miss Mary's party, I'm guilty of not using my common sense. Go on up to the back door. Ask for Tony.''

"Thanks,'' Johnny told the guard.

The hood nodded, thinking he was being thanked for letting Johnny in. He didn't suspect that the thanks was for the free information.

Ten seconds after Johnny rang the back doorbell, the heavy door was opened by a beefy giant wearing a plain white chef's apron.

"Guy at the gate told me to ask for Tony,'' Johnny explained.

"Yeah. What do you want?'' The man had a low, big voice to go with his size.

Johnny rolled his eyes. "Got an order of beer for Schizzetto. What do I do with them?''

"Put them in the cooler downstairs and beat it!''

"Yes, sir,'' Johnny replied in a timid voice. He found the light switch, then picked up two cases of beer and carried them down a dark flight of stairs.

Johnny breathed a sigh of relief. He had done some good guessing so far, but his luck couldn't last much longer. All he had intended to do was get inside the door and start cracking heads until he found some weapons.

It seemed reasonable that any house with hard force had plenty of weapons hidden somewhere. A young woman lived in the house so there was a good chance her parties would be held in a rumpus room in the basement; and the basement was the only place to look for a small weapons firing range. With all the soldiers around, they'd have to practice somewhere.

His first guess proved correct. The stairs led him to a large room with a bar at one end. Behind the bar was a cooler that would easily hold six cases of beer. It was full. If someone checked, it would blow the hell out of his beer delivery story.

Johnny set down the beer and looked around. Only two doors led out of the rec room. The first one led to a laundry room. There was a furnace in the background. The second door was locked. Johnny snapped his foot forward at waist height, smashing out one of the door panels. A quick glance confirmed his second guess; there was a professional-looking firing range on the other side of the door.

Tony was stomping down the stairs with all the finesse of a Clydesdale. Johnny glanced quickly around the basement room, but there was nothing handy that he could use as a weapon.

BOLAN LAY FLAT ON HIS BACK, too weak to stand without assistance, while a young prostitute stripped off her dressing gown and prepared to go to bed with him.

Naked, freshly showered and without her heavy makeup, Melody Mergims stood before Bolan. She was transformed from something tawdry into a fine example of the female human animal. Her body was slim, her breasts small and firm, her muscles well defined. She had the body of an athlete.

The damp hair and unpainted face made her look adolescent. Normally, another ten years and her youthful looks would make her the envy of other women, but another ten years as a hooker would leave only a burnt-out skeleton.

The way she stood by the bed did nothing for Bolan's libido. She displayed herself like a grocer carefully piling up his best produce. Bolan could see that Melody's use of her own body had already depreciated its value in her own eyes.

As Megrims lifted the covers and slid in next to Bolan's naked body, his sense of reality underwent further trauma. He was took weak to have much desire for her. But perhaps because she reminded him somehow of his dead sister, his heart cried with the urge to hold her and comfort her, to let her know that no matter what happened, she had as much value as she was willing to allow herself.

Melody snuggled up to him, laying her head on his good shoulder and letting her fingernails trail tantalizingly across his lower abdomen. Bolan wrapped his good arm around her and pulled her to him, allowing her hands too little room to maneuver. They lay like that for five minutes.

"I didn't think you were too weak to enjoy some gentle lovemaking," she said at last.

"I'm not."

"Then what are we waiting for?"

"Another time. Another place. Maybe another world. I don't know."

She pushed herself away from him and almost fell in her haste to get out of the bed. She stood over him, her shoulders shaking, but her eyes dry.

"A whore's not good enough for you!"

"I didn't say that. I didn't think that."

But she was beyond hearing what was actually said. She stomped around, angrily pulling on clothing. "Take care of yourself for a while. Mr. High and Mighty," she shouted, then slammed the door and stamped her feet all the way down two flights of stairs.

When Melody Megrims strode into the kitchen, Edgar Twichen and Patricia Dane had their heads together over the kitchen table. Megrims had never seen them talking so seriously, as if they were dealing with a major crisis. When they saw Melody, they jumped apart like two kids caught playing doctor.

"How's the patient?" Dane asked, much too sweetly.

Megrims poured herself a large mug of coffee from the percolator. If either Patricia or Eddy made it, it was bound to be awful, but Melody was in a mood to subject herself to awful things.

"If you mean that self-righteous prick, Cancellari, he's resting smugly, thank you." Megrims's voice was so bitter that the other two both glanced at her sharply, and then exchanged puzzled frowns.

Twichen finally said, "Johnny wasn't such a pain in the ass until that guy showed up. Cancellari's the one who's got him acting like no one else counts."

In her present mood, Melody wanted to hear anything that reflected badly on anyone else. She knew that she wanted to make others seem small, because she felt so small herself. But knowing that didn't lessen her desire to see others brought down to her own level.

"What's Johnny done now?" she asked.

The two were brimming over with indignation to the point where they both tried to answer at once. They paused, both started again and stopped simultaneously. On the third attempt, Dane was the first to speak.

"Johnny told me that if those vigilantes on the street attack me, it's my fault because of the way I dress. What right has he to criticize the way I dress!"

"Perhaps he just didn't want to see you beat up," Melody murmured, but her comment was lost under Twichen's aggrieved complaint.

"The evening when that Cancellari guy arrived, Johnny caught me with a surprise punch when I didn't answer a question quickly enough. You'd think he had some right to my answers!" Twichen's voice rose in indignation. He caught a breath and continued, "I'm going to get him by surprise tonight. We'll see how that bastard likes being punched out for no reason at all."

"That should certainly be something to see," Melody murmured.

She leaned back and sipped her coffee. She felt better just thinking of Twichen and Johnny Gray making asses of themselves in a fight. She had no idea who would win. Twichen had the better physique, but she had a feeling that Johnny, who was supposed to be bringing something back for Corsaro, knew his way around and would be far from helpless. It would be quite a contest.

9

Johnny ran to the foot of the stairs to catch Tony before he could see what was happening and get set for battle. The big chef was stomping down the stairs, not expecting trouble. He saw Johnny and opened his mouth to speak, but never got the words out.

While Tony was still three steps from the bottom of the stairs, a straight left jab to the crotch ended the fight before it began. As Tony jackknifed down the last few steps, the hard edge of Johnny's open right hand caught him at the base of his skull, putting him to sleep.

Johnny dragged the unconscious form to one side, but didn't bother trying to hide it. He was running out of time. He had to take what weapons he could find and get out before it was too late.

He ran into the indoor firing range, and moved straight to the elaborate, ten-foot-long gun cabinet and tried the doors. They were locked. Johnny glanced around the room, but could see nothing he could use to force the doors.

Someone was calling Tony's name, but the chef was still in dreamland. Soon they would look downstairs.

Johnny dashed through the rec room into the combination laundry and furnace room. He found a small but well-equipped workbench in one corner. He snatched up a short crowbar and a large screwdriver and ran back to the gun cabinet. As he passed back through the rec room, the voice calling for Tony seemed to be closer to the top of the stairs.

The crowbar made quick work of the cabinet, but showed little respect for the fine walnut finish. Inside were enough guns to outfit a dedicated survivalist group. The expensive, well-kept weapons each had spare magazines and boxes of ammunition.

The first weapons to catch his attention were two of the rare Swiss MP-44 submachine guns. To make sure his memory was correct, Johnny checked the rounds in one of the clips. The submachine guns used 9 mm parabellums, the same ammunition as Mack needed for his Beretta.

A quick scan of the handguns produced a Japanese Nambu Model 57-A, a good automatic that also used 9 mm parabellums. The magazine already had a full eight-round load.

Johnny flipped off the thumb safety and returned to the recreation room once again. He untied Tony's large apron and rolled the unconscious man out of it. Two voices were hollering for Tony. One was at the head of the stairs.

Back in the firing range, Johnny threw the apron on the floor. He tucked the automatic in his belt and put one of the Swiss SMGs on the apron. There were nine spare box magazines. He dumped those on the apron. He could find no extra clips for the Nambu, but there was no more time to look. Someone was coming down the stairs.

Johnny added a case of parabellum ammo to the pile on the apron. He then picked up the corners of the cloth with his left hand, tossing the load over his shoulder. He scooped up the second MP-44 in his hand, awkwardly chambered the first round and raced out of the gun room.

A guy came roaring down the stairs, shouting orders. Johnny suspected that Schizzetto's head cook had been caught napping. He wore old-fashioned suspenders, only one of which was up; he was struggling to get the other one over his shoulder holster. Also, he wore no shoes; he was in his socks. Schizzetto was only five foot three and his chief of security was no larger. He skidded to a stop when he saw the MP-44 in Johnny's hand.

He clawed frantically at the Colt .45 in his shoulder holster. As he started to pull the weapon, he also started to say, "Oh, sh..."

Johnny lightly stroked the trigger of the submachine gun. A three-round burst knocked the shit from the tip of the mobster's tongue out the back of his head. The tongue went with it.

Johnny didn't miss a pace. He leaped over the body and took the stairs two at a time. Shouts filled the house. Someone put his head around the doorway from the kitchen. A short burst, and the head pulled back.

Johnny dashed out of the house, placed his load in the back of the Volkswagen, slammed the side door and jumped into the driver's seat. Then he took it easy around the corner of the house and down the drive. No one in the house seemed to associate the slowly moving van with the trouble indoors.

When he stopped at the gate, Johnny told the gatekeeper in guard's uniform, "Boy, am I in trouble!"

The gatekeeper cocked an eyebrow.

"This great big guy in a white apron came to the door. I carried the beer downstairs, then he asked if I liked Italian food. I told him it was too greasy. He started shouting and shooting; I got the hell out."

The guard looked at Johnny's white tense face and broke out laughing. As he opened the gate, he said, "You better get out of here, kid, and if I were you, I wouldn't come back. You're just too stupid to live."

Johnny didn't answer. He floored the accelerator and got the hell away from the Don's hardsite.

On his way back to the Mafia teen trap in downtown Vancouver, Johnny stopped and bought a secondhand suitcase. He filled it with the two submachine guns, the Nambu from his belt and the ammunition. With the suitcase safely on the seat beside him, he drove two figure eights to make sure he wasn't being followed. Then he made tracks back to his brother.

Johnny walked in the front door, straight into a fist in the gut. He doubled over, dropping the suitcase. His first thought was one of thanks that the blow hadn't been four inches higher; it would have killed him. Then he began to wonder how the Mafia knew enough to be here, waiting for him.

"You don't seem to do very well on the receiving end of a surprise punch," Twichen sneered.

Slowly, Johnny forced himself to stand straight. "Oh, it's you," he said. He actually felt relieved. "I hope that makes you feel better."

Johnny bent forward to retrieve the suitcase, but was stopped by a hard hook to the side of the head. He staggered against the wall rather than fall down. The car keys fell from his other hand.

"You don't seem to like your own medicine very much," Twichen crowed.

"That's showing him!" Dane sneered.

Johnny pulled himself erect once more, shaking his head to clear the cobwebs. He could see Dane and Megrims farther down the hall. They were watching Twichen with savage intensity.

"You've made your point," Johnny told Twichen. "You should be satisfied now."

As soon as he said the words, Johnny realized that Twichen was feeling far too satisfied. It was a bit late for insights, but Johnny could see that Twichen's smug self-satisfactions formed a thin, brittle shell over an ego that felt powerless all too often. Now Twichen believed he was administering a beating; it was a power trip he wouldn't give up easily.

Johnny deflected an uppercut that was aimed at his chin.

"Stand up and fight like a man," Twichen bellowed.

Johnny felt overwhelming desperation. It would be easy to clobber this idiot, but he didn't dare. If Twichen started nursing a grudge, he could get looselipped about Mack. The porn actor could even decide to give Mack a beating as well. And Mack was too weak to stand, let alone take on this immature whirlwind of anger and fear. On the other hand, not striking back was only firing up his anger and sense of power. Twichen was young and well muscled. Johnny couldn't take many of his awkward punches.

Johnny put his shoulder to Twichen's chest and drove him backward. When they were opposite the mattress-covered living room, Johnny's right fist slammed to his opponent's ribs, driving him into the room. Twichen staggered through the doorway from the impact of the right hook. Before he could recover his balance, he tripped on the edge of a mattress and went down.

Johnny fell on top of him, pinning his shoulders. Johnny's idea was to smother resistance until he could talk some sense into Eddy. But Johnny had forgotten that mattress contortions were Twichen's specialty. Long legs snaked up, wrapped around Johnny's and yanked. Johnny was forced off Twichen. Both fighters regained their feet.

Twichen was both angry and frightened. There was an explosive violence to his movements that could easily kill or maim. Normally, Johnny Bolan Gray could use his Marine training and easily handle an inexperienced fighter like Twichen. But it would be a mistake to damage Twichen and a worse one to humiliate him. For Mack's sake, Johnny wanted to get out of this fight unscathed and still leave Twichen's frail ego intact.

Johnny ignored Twichen's flailing fists and put one hand on each of his opponent's knees. He dug his thumbs in just above the knee caps, while exerting pressure to slip the legs over his head. Twichen let out a sudden squeal of pain and Johnny released the pressure.

Johnny rolled away and slowly rose to his feet. Twichen sprang up, high on the thought that he was cleansing himself of many humiliations by beating Johnny.

From the doorway, Dane said, "Way to go!"

Johnny spared a quick glance and took in two pale faces. He tried to figure out if the "Way to go!" was an encouragement for Twichen or a celebration of the fight itself. Either way, it disgusted him.

"Don't you think we're old enough to settle this more calmly?" he asked Twichen.

"I'm going to throw you out of here, one piece at a time," Twichen grunted.

Twichen charged in like a windmill, his head down and his arms flailing. Johnny stepped to one side and pushed him sideways into the wall. Blocking the doorway, Johnny landed two solid body punches that blasted the wind out of Twichen's lungs. The young prince of porn could only prop himself against the wall and gasp for air.

Johnny retreated until his back touched the opposite wall. He leaned back as if exhausted.

"Enough," he told Twichen. "You win."

"Not enough! Not until I throw you out of here."

Johnny couldn't believe his ears. Didn't Twichen realize he'd been beaten? How could he help someone that stupid to save face?

Twichen pushed himself off the wall and staggered over to Johnny. His fists were low and Johnny was tempted to smash his nose. However, the young actor was vain about his looks. He was also in the midst of making another porn film. It would be unwise to rearrange his features at this time. The Mob could start asking questions.

Johnny blocked Twichen's wild punches, slowly backing away from the door. Twichen followed, arms flailing, but no real weight behind the fists. Still some punches got through and they stung. When Twichen's body was between Johnny and the faces in the doorway, Johnny hammered home three more hard blows to the stomach. Twichen folded up like a Chinese fan.

Johnny supported Twichen back to the wall. Holding Twichen up, Johnny said, "You're a tough fighter, Eddy. I've had enough."

This time, Twichen had no illusions about winning. He was still trying to persuade his diaphragm to pump air and his face was a study in agony. It took him another thirty seconds before he could push away from Johnny and stand on his own. This was long enough for him to realize that he had really lost the fight, even though Johnny was the one who spoke of giving up.

"Yeah," Twichen gasped. Then he turned and staggered from the room.

Dane was waiting in the hall with open arms. Her eyes were dilated with excitement.

"Come on up to my room," she whispered hoarsely.

"Not now," Twichen answered, rubbing his stomach. "We better save it until tomorrow. We got a big scene to do."

"That's not the same thing!" Dane wailed.

"It is for me," Twichen mumbled leaving by the front door.

"You call that a fight?" Mergrims said softly as Johnny returned to the hall.

"I don't call it anything," Johnny answered.

He looked around for the secondhand suitcase, containing the weapons. It was gone.

Johnny dashed out the front door to see if Twichen had the weapons. Twichen was leaning against the porch railing, still fighting to get his wind back. A quick inspection of the porch, street and abbreviated front yard showed no sign of either the suitcase or the weapons it contained.

Johnny burst back into the house. The two women were gone. One pair of female feet clattered on the bare stairs. He looked in the hall closet. Nothing. Nor did the kitchen yield the missing weapons.

He took the stairs three at a time, wondering which woman went upstairs and where the other went. By the time he reached the second floor, the footsteps were in the third floor hall. Johnny reached the top floor in time to see Patricia Dane enter the room he shared with Mack and Melody. Dane's hands were empty.

"I'm Patricia Dane..." she began.

"Pat, have you seen Melody?" Johnny interrupted.

"I left her downstairs," she answered. There was frost in her voice.

Johnny didn't wait to find out what that was about. Mack could cope with the great actress for a few minutes. Johnny retraced his steps, looking for Melody.

This time, he found Melody out on the porch, talking to Twichen. There was still no trace of the suitcase. When Johnny stepped outside, the two stopped talking and stared at him.

"Either of you seen the suitcase I had when I came in?"
Johnny asked.

"What suitcase?" Twichen asked.

"I didn't see any suitcase," Melody said.

10

Bolan still spent most of his time sleeping as his body fought the infection and tried to rebuild itself. The last few days had passed in a haze with only occasional clear patches. Usually the clarity took place when emergency caused his body to pump adrenaline. So when a gentle knock on the door woke him, Bolan was pleased to find he was relatively alert, even though there didn't appear to be an emergency at the moment.

A young woman stepped into the room without waiting for her knock to be acknowledged.

"I'm Patricia Dane."

She was interrupted by Johnny's voice from the hall. Bolan was relieved to hear it, but puzzled that Johnny didn't come right in. He'd left in search of weapons. What had happened?

"I left her downstairs," Dane called over her shoulder to Johnny, her voice unfriendly.

She closed the door before Bolan could call out to Johnny, and glided across the room to perch gingerly on the edge of Bolan's bed. She was a study in confused thinking. She had the face and figure of an immature girl, but she moved and spoke like a woman in her late twenties. Her makeup was a blatant attempt to look older. Bolan wondered if the deception worked on other people. All it did for him was remind him of a small girl dressing up.

She wore clothing he would have expected to see on a business woman in her forties. However, Patricia Dane wore them in her own unique way. The plain white blouse was worn without underwear, and her nipples were clearly visible beneath the sheer nylon. The dark split skirt looked dated because it was worn over mesh stocking. The four-inch high heels were the final cheapening touch. However, she wore the clothes with such confidence that Bolan could not imagine her in anything else.

"So you're Johnny Gray's big brother," she began.

Bolan nodded and waited.

"You know he came chasing up here after me? I hardly even know him."

Bolan considered that an interesting way to describe the situation, but refused to rise to the bait. Whatever Dane wanted, she could get around to it in her own way.

"You don't say much, do you?"

"Hello," he answered. "I'm Corsaro Cancellari. Pleased to meet you."

She smiled. "I guess I am getting to the point faster than people usually do, but I'm just like that. Besides, your name isn't really Corsaro Cancellari."

"What led you to decide that?"

"I'm not stupid! Johnny works at the Free Legal Aid Center in San Diego. That's where I'm from. Sandy Darlow was a friend of mine. I imagine that's how my family came to send him after me. But I'm not going back and he can't make me. I'm beginning to build a career here.

"Anyway, Johnny was Johnny Gray in San Diego and he's Johnny Gray here. So how can someone called Corsaro Cancellari be his brother?"

Bolan smiled at her. "Not everyone is as proud of having Mafia connections as you are."

"I don't have Mafia connections!"

Bolan's smile faded in a split second, causing Dane to lean away from him.

"Who signs your paycheck?"

"Just because Mr. Hanchovini's Italian doesn't mean he's a mobster."

"We don't like the words 'mob' and 'mobster.' You better learn to call us 'family.' You got that?" Bolan's voice had a nasty edge to it.

Patricia Dane's relaxed attitude vanished. She sat tensely on the edge of the bed, eyeing Bolan as if she expected him to explode.

Bolan changed his voice from hard to oily, as if he were trying to soothe her but didn't really care enough to work at it.

"Don't worry about Johnny. The kid's young yet; he still thinks he can buck the organization. I'll have a talk with him. He won't try to get you to go home again. Just don't pay him any attention, kid. You keep on making those films."

Bolan paused and leaned forward to stare at her face intently. Then he leaned back on his pillow. When he continued speaking, it was through a lopsided grin. "You got a good face. When you're too old for this kiddy porn stuff, you'll do good as a hooker. You got it made."

"I'm never going to be a hooker," she told him. Her voice quivered from anger and humiliation. "I'm going to be a great actress."

"Yeah. Sure. An actress. Whatever you say. Just don't pay any attention to Johnny. I'm not so weak I can't take care of that punk."

Dane stared at Bolan. Her lips were trembling. By acting the part of a hoodlum, Bolan had managed to give her a small glimpse of her real future with the Mob. He knew he was gambling, but he was sure that if he simply tried to reason with her, he would be no more successful than Johnny had been.

"Is he really your brother?" Dane asked. She was making conversation while trying to figure out Cancellari's real angle.

"Yeah, but he's not family. Not yet."

"What's that mean?"

Bolan ignored the question. "You're sort of sexy at that," he told her. "When I'm feeling better, I'll give you a night you'll never forget."

"I am not a whore!" she shouted.

"Of course not. But I'm a visiting producer. You wouldn't turn down a producer, would you?"

The stricken look on Dane's face told Bolan he'd hit the mark. He wondered how many times Frankie Hanky had sent her to bed with a visiting mobster, telling her that she was pleasing a producer. When Bolan got out of that bed, he had something to settle with that purveyor of children, and with his boss.

Bolan had no chance to further Patricia Dane's insights into the hell she was walking into. The door opened and Eddy Twichen entered without knocking.

"What's happening?" he asked.

"Mr. Cancellari's being nasty," Dane informed him. "He says the Mafia owns Lion's Gate Productions, that we're working for the Mafia."

"So what's new?"

"You mean you agree with him?"

"Who else could afford all the big film stuff? Who else could distribute the stuff? You know that," Twichen told her.

It was obvious to Bolan, as it was not to Twichen, that Patricia Dane had not let herself know that she knew that.

She wanted to see herself as a famous actress; being a tool of the Cosa Nostra didn't fit that image.

Her face stiffened as she fought back tears and the reality that threatened to overcome her. "You can lie about our employers all you like, but don't include me. I don't believe either of you."

She tried to push past Twichen, who stopped her with an arm around her shoulder.

"Come on, Patty. It's not all that bad. We're valuable to them. Where else could we earn the type of money we're earning now?"

"Money! Is that all you care about? Why don't you just go out on the street and peddle your ass, like Melody? Let go of me."

"Hey. What did this guy say to upset you? We've got another big scene to do tomorrow. If Mr. Hanchovini finds that he's been upsetting you before a big scene, he'll settle his hash." Twichen finished his speech with a nasty glance at Bolan.

Dane replied by swinging a small hard fist into Twichen's midsection. Normally, the blow wouldn't have bothered him, but Johnny had already tenderized the area. Twichen let out a gasp and doubled over as Dane marched out of the room.

Twichen straightened slowly, giving Bolan a murderous stare. His face was beet red. Bolan didn't need to be told that Twichen's macho self-image was badly dented by the blow to the plexus.

"What are you staring at?" Twichen demanded.

"A man having a fight with his ego."

"Is that supposed to mean something?"

"It means I can't figure you out. I'm looking for clues."

Twichen's curiosity was caught. "What's there to figure?

"You're a complex person. You walk around as if you were simple, but you see reality better than most of the people around you. How do you manage to both see reality and ignore it, too?"

"What are you selling?"

"Honesty. Try some."

"No thanks. People who sell honesty really want confessions. I've got nothing to confess."

"Not to me, but what about confessing to yourself?"

"You're playing games with words."

"No," Bolan told him. "You are. You act so casual when you point out to Patricia that she's working for the Mob, but you don't seem to have gone on to look at what that's going to mean for either of you in the future."

"As I said, we're valuable property."

"For how long?"

Melody Megrims came into the room, saving Twichen from having to think about the last question.

"Hi," she said. Her manner was much too casual.

"Where have you been?" Twichen said. "Johnny was looking for you."

"Well, I certainly haven't been looking for him. I see too much of him as it is. Were you two having man talk, or can anyone join in?"

"I was just leaving."

"Then it was man talk. I stayed out while Patty was visiting. I didn't want to embarrass anyone." She looked coldly at Bolan while she spoke. "But I didn't know you two had secrets to share."

"We don't. I was really on my way out," Twichen snapped at her.

"Patricia giving you a hard time? And just after you turned her down, too. I think you blew your big chance, lover boy."

"Shut up!"

Melody suddenly shifted tack, her voice gentle. "Don't let her get to you, Eddy. She's not worth it."

"Shut your mouth! What would a whore like you know about who's worth it and who's not?"

Melody stood with a white face and clenched fists, while Twichen stomped out of the room and slammed the door.

"Damn," she whispered.

"He's upset," Bolan remarked.

"This seems to be my day for being put in my place," Melody said. She was still struggling to hold back tears.

"Yes it does," Bolan agreed.

"This going to be a sermon about my way of life?"

Bolan shook his head. "A sermon about taking personally things that have nothing to do with you."

"So it's all my fault. I knew it would come to that."

Bolan was beginning to feel tired again. Yet Melody still tore at his heart. What could he say or do to persuade her to help herself?

"Yes, it's your fault," he told her.

Before she could say anything, there was a light knock on the door and Johnny let himself in.

"What's wrong?" Bolan asked.

Johnny glanced at Melody and said nothing.

"She's staking everything on us. Shouldn't she know what she's getting into?" Bolan asked.

"It isn't safe for her to know."

"They'll assume she knows. Why not ask her?"

Megrims stood quietly while Johnny and Mack talked. She was attentive, but relaxed.

"If you mean you two have been playing fast and loose with the Mob, that isn't news. Anyone can see you're not who you say you are," she told them.

Johnny weighed things in his own mind, before asking, "You sure you want to know?"

"If I'm going to get the treatment, I'd like to know why."

Johnny stated the facts bluntly. "We needed weapons. So I went to Schizzetto's and borrowed a few. The guard at the gate saw my face and will remember me. So will the chef."

Bolan was thunderstruck. "You went in there alone? What sort of intelligence did you have?"

"I looked the place over for about an hour. We needed the weapons. I didn't want to waste time."

"What went wrong?" Bolan asked.

"Other than leaving witnesses, you mean? Nothing, except when I walked in the front door here. Twichen decided that he had to have it out with me. By the time Eddy and I had come to an amicable settlement, the suitcase with the weapons was gone."

"Where did this happen?"

"Right downstairs." Johnny shrugged. "Whoever took that suitcase isn't exactly a friend. The only thing I've succeeded in doing is arming our enemies."

Melody looked from one man to the other, confused. Suddenly she broke into tears and ran from the room.

"What's wrong with her?" Johnny asked.

"Just confused," Bolan answered. "The real question is what's wrong with you? That raid on Schizzetto's was risky. You didn't have time to make a proper recon before you went in."

"The recon showed a hardsite. I went in on bluff. We needed the weapons and that was the only place I knew to get them. Now, I've got to go back again, tonight."

"That's suicide," Bolan told him. "You've got more sense than that."

Johnny grinned at his elder brother. "If I have, I'm hiding it well. How could I possibly get suckered into a brawl while the weapons walked away?"

"You did what you thought was best each step of the way. You want to do better than that?" Bolan demanded. His voice was harsh.

Johnny was brought up short by the hard edge to Mack's voice. He paused for a moment, then grinned.

"I guess I was feeling sorry for myself. I'll just have to go back for more. At least they won't be expecting that."

"They'll be expecting just that. Instead, why don't you do a top to bottom search of the house? Unless Patricia, Melody or Edgar have left the house, the odds are that your suitcase of guns is somewhere around here, too."

"You suspect one of them?"

"If not all three. Someone from outside the house seems unlikely."

"Why?"

Bolan shrugged.

"I'll look. In the meantime, we're sitting ducks."

Bolan sympathized, but there was no way he could make it easier for Johnny. He'd have to make the best of a grim situation until they found who their friends were and who their enemies were.

All the visitors and conversation had exhausted Bolan. There was nothing he could do. So he rolled over and went to sleep.

Johnny stood looking down at his brother. Mack was too sick to get out of bed, but still kept cool. Johnny shook his head with admiration and left the room, looking for the suitcase. All hell would break loose soon.

He *had* to find weapons.

11

Patricia Dane was shaking with anger when she left Bolan. He had no right to make her feel cheap simply because she was doing what had to be done in order to have a movie career.

In spite of her anger, a small voice kept telling her that she had no guarantee that Hanchovini would ever find her a legitimate film part. She paced the downstairs hall, trying to shake her anger and her feelings of uncertainty.

She stopped and looked at her watch. Hanchovini would still be at the studio. He usually came in late and worked late. Patricia Dane knew how she could assure herself a legitimate movie career. She ran back upstairs to her room and retrieved her purse. She then left the house.

Eddy Twichen arrived on the main floor just as Dane closed the front door. The last crack of light from the closing door spotlighted the car keys Johnny had dropped when Twichen hit him for the second time.

Twichen scooped up the keys and opened the door carefully. As soon as Dane was well down the sidewalk, Twichen darted out of the house and into Johnny's bus. He started the engine and moved out slowly, intent on following Dane. If he had been asked why, he could not have answered. There was just something about the furtiveness of her movement that made him feel it would be worthwhile to follow her.

Dane found a taxi when she reached Hastings Street, making Twichen glad he had "borrowed" Johnny's Volkswagen. It took him very little time to discern that the taxi was headed back to Lion's Gate Productions. He had no idea why she'd return to the studio, but he was determined to find out.

Twichen knew several shortcuts, but he didn't depend solely on his knowledge of Vancouver to reach the studio before Dane's taxi. He cut corners, ran two stop signs and a red light. After all, the car wasn't his. Twichen was content to have Johnny answer as many summonses for traffic violations as possible. It would serve the bastard right! Twichen decided that if he had an accident, he'd simply walk away and let Johnny worry.

He was inside the door of the studio and out of sight when Dane came in. It was a simple matter to follow her through the darkened halls to Hanchovini's office. He seemed to be the only one left in the building. Dane gave a perfunctory rap on the jamb of the open door and walked in. From the shadows, Twichen watched Dane sit down on the studio boss's desk.

"What brings you back here?" Hanchovini growled.

Twichen could not see Dane's smile, but he knew it was there from the tone of her voice when she said, "Well, you *are* going to get me into a Hollywood picture, aren't you, Mr. Hanchovini?

"Listen, Miss Dane. I don't have time for this now."

Twichen was suddenly struck by the obviousness of Hanchovini's manipulative style. The studio boss always called him Eddy, making him feel like one of the boys. Patricia was always Miss Dane, and that seemed to fit her need to be treated as someone special.

Other than being careful how he addressed them, Hanchovini treated all the young porn stars with indifference or contempt. The insight did nothing to improve Twichen's self-image. He compensated by feeling angrier at Corsaro and his brother.

"I understand you're a very busy man, Mr. Hanchovini."

Twichen smiled at how thick Patricia Dane laid it on.

"But I just wanted to make sure you're doing your best to help me, because I'm doing my best to help you. That's why I'm here."

"Get to the point," Hanchovini snapped.

"The point is very simple. Johnny Gray is really Johnny Gray. He works for the Free Legal Aid Center in San Diego. I know him from there."

Twichen could hear the laughter in Dane's voice as she dropped her bombshell. "So how come he's the brother of your friend, Mr. Cancellari? Someone isn't who he says he is and those two seem awfully anxious to pull me out of this picture before it's finished."

There was a moment's silence. Then Hanchovini was speaking on the telephone.

"Salvatori, this is Frankie. Is The Picker there...? Who else was asking...? What the hell does Little Squirt's security want with The Picker...? Nah, I can't guess either....

"Too bad I missed him but it's a small favor. Will you take care of it for me, right away, Sal...? Yeah, you know the house I got on Jackson Street? There's a guy there with a couple bullets in his shoulder called Cancellari, and another one—young punk named Gray. I want you and one of the boys to go down and talk to them. Then check out their story. Check them out real close. If there's anything wrong, you know what to do with them.... Thanks, Sal."

Twichen did not wait to hear the phone being hung up. He stole out of the studios and back to the bus. It would be too damn dangerous to be caught eavesdropping. Besides, if he hurried he'd be back in time to see this Salvatori and his friend shake the hell out of Cancellari and Gray. Those two made Twichen very uncomfortable. He smiled at the thought of seeing them worked over. He drove just as recklessly on the way back as he had going to the studio.

JOHNNY EMERGED from the third-floor bedroom in time to hear someone walk in the front door and start up the stairs. Johnny hastened to intercept whoever it was. He intercepted Pico "The Picker" Pellico in the second-floor hall. The *mafioso* was wearing his usual sweatshirt and greasy ponytail.

"He awake?" the Picker asked.

Johnny had decided he wouldn't leave Mack alone with any of the Mafia unless he was sure his brother was alert. He couldn't ask The Picker his business, but Johnny would make sure he was present when The Picker faced Mack. Until Mack was stronger, it was essential that no one catch him off guard.

Johnny gave The Picker a deferential smile. "No, but his orders are that I'm to wake him if you show up. Give me a minute, huh? He feels a little off stride when he first wakes up."

Johnny didn't wait for the hood to reply, but turned and headed for the bedroom, leaving Pellico to follow him. Johnny slipped in the door and closed it behind him. Mack was sound asleep. Johnny shook his brother.

"Wake up, Mack."

Bolan's eyes slowly focused on Johnny. He felt like weeping. Mack used to wake instantly. There seemed to be no period of disorientation between the time he was asleep and the time he was awake. But the wound had been serious and the healing process seemed to require strength that Bolan no longer had.

The cold blue eyes focused in a matter of seconds; to Johnny it seemed like an eternity.

"What's wrong?" Bolan aksed.

"Pellico's here to see you."

"Help me sit up." Bolan's command left no room for argument.

Pellico moved quietly into the room while Johnny helped his brother upright in bed and propped a pillow behind him. The Picker hooked a sneaker around a chair leg, pulled the chair over and straddled it, his arms resting on the chair back.

"The wound seems to have taken a lot out of you, Corsaro." Pellico's voice was thoughtful.

Bolan ignored the comment and turned to Johnny. "You've got something to do, kid."

"Yeah, but..."

"But nothing. Find that thing. It's important. Besides, my friend and I want to talk."

Johnny was uneasy, but it would look strange if he didn't follow orders. And of course, Mack was right. They needed to find those weapons and to find out which of the occupants of the house had it in for them. Johnny decided to start on the main floor and work his way up.

He began with the closet near the front door. He'd already searched there twice, but it would be the natural hiding place for something hurriedly snatched from the hall. This time he brought a chair from the kitchen, set it inside the large closet and stepped up on it. With the closet door wide open, there was just enough light to examine the dust on the top shelf. The hall closet had been the first stop. Where had it gone from there?

Before Johnny could answer his own question, the front door crashed open, colliding with the closet door and banging it shut. Johnny eased himself off the chair before pushing the door open a crack.

Two men stood with their backs to him, holstered revolvers on their hips. Johnny recognized the uniforms as being the same as those worn by the guards around Schizzetto's place. When one of the men spoke, Johnny knew it was the man who'd been on the gate when he'd raided Schizzetto's for weapons earlier in the day. He could scarcely have missed the van out front.

"No one here," grunted the gatekeeper.

"The hookers will all be on the street by now," his friend answered, "but Sal said The Picker would be here. Let's take a look around."

"Hell! I'll save us some time." The guy from the gate bellowed, "Picker." His voice was loud enough to reach upstairs, two blocks over.

In a moment, Picker's voice came down from the top of the stairs. "That you, Chop Chop? What you want?"

"Sal said I'd find you here. It's important."

"Come on up."

Johnny didn't like the situation in the least. He wasn't sure how Schizzetto's security had traced him to the house so quickly, but it didn't look good. That he was still unarmed didn't do anything to lift Johnny's spirits. He stole from the closet and followed the two Mafia security up the stairs.

Johnny was looking around the edge of the staircase when The Picker motioned the two uniformed men into Bolan's presence. As soon as the door closed, he tiptoed to the door to hear what was happening.

He had no trouble hearing Picker's harsh voice say, "Well, Chop Chop, what the fuck are you and Mario doing here?"

There was a pause. Picker continued the conversation. "This is C.C. His full handle's Corsaro Cancellari. He's here from New York on business when someone put a couple of slugs into him. You can talk in front of C.C.; he's family, and a friend. So what are you after?"

There was another pause before Chop Chop said, "I'm in deep shit, Picker, and I need your help."

"So, shoot."

"Earlier today, a young punk came to the gate, claiming to be making a beer delivery. He seemed legit, so I let him through. He knocked out Big Tony, stole a bunch of guns, then drove back out past me as cool as *gelato*.

"Little Squirt's out of town, but if I don't have that punk sewn up by the time he gets back, I'll probably be going swimming in a cement bathing suit."

Pellico's voice suddenly became frosty. No one in the organization would dare befriend anyone on his way for a final swim. "So what do you want from me?"

"As I said, the guy's a young punk. You know most of the junior garbage in the burg. I'm hoping that when I describe him, you'll know him."

"So, shoot."

"He's in his early twenties. Wears glasses. Same size I am, five foot ten. Dark hair, blue eyes, skinny. Hair sort of long, but not as long as these hippy kids wear it. He drives a blue Volkswagen bus, if he didn't steal the thing special for the job."

Bolan's voice cut in, quiet, authoritative. "I'll handle this, Pico. I know who you're after. One of my boys, my best. He'd have gone through you one way or another, so don't feel bad."

"Don't feel bad!" The shout went up a full octave. "I'm going to get wasted because of you? I'm going to have a pair of heads waiting for Mr. Schizzetto and yours will be one of them.''

''Maybe, if you heard the rest of it,'' Bolan said mildly.

''No way. Now, out of that bed.''

Johnny didn't wait to hear any more. He rushed through the door. Mack was in danger and Johnny had no thought left for himself.

When the door flew open, both men whirled to face it, guns drawn. Their reactions weren't quick enough. Johnny launched himself in a high dive, grabbing a neck in each hand. The weapons didn't have time to find a target before the two heads were smashed together.

The guard who did the least talking had his gun halfway around. His finger instinctively tightened on the trigger, putting a bullet into Chop Chop's abdomen.

There wasn't time for another shot. Johnny shifted his left hand from the wounded hood to his companion's chin. With his left hand on the chin and his right on the neck, he gave a sudden twisting jerk, his wiry muscles bulging from the effort. The result sounded loud in the small room. For one mobster, the trip to hell had been a snap.

Chop Chop had his left hand over the wound in his abdomen. He was unaware that his intestines were flowing from an eight-inch hole in his back. All his concentration was on his right hand, which had swung his Colt revolver to aim at Johnny's gut. The finger was right on the trigger.

Before the gun went off, Pico Pellico kicked it to one side. The bullet buried itself harmlessly in the wall. All Chop Chop's effort had gone into that shot. He dropped the revolver and collapsed.

''Get something under him, Johnny. We can't afford to leave blood stains,'' Bolan said.

Then Bolan turned his attention to Pellico, who was aiming a Browning Hi-Power at his head.

"You better have a good explanation for this, C.C."

Bolan leaned back on the pillow and smiled weakly. "The best."

Johnny rolled Chop Chop's corpse in a scatter rug from beside Melody's bed. While he worked, he slid the dead man's Colt next to his leg. Pellico swung the Browning automatic to cover Johnny.

"Just leave the gun where it is," The Picker advised him.

Johnny carefully backed away from the Colt. Pellico shifted his small snake eyes back to Bolan.

"I don't think you can talk your way out of this one, C.C."

"I sent him to take every weapon in the joint that fired 9 mm parabellums," Bolan told Pellico. "That's what was dug out of my shoulder. The guns are already on the way to a friend for ballistics, but that's just proof for back east. I already know what I know. That's why Little Cock ain't around anymore to protect Little Squirt."

"Little Cock always uses...used a big cannon."

Bolan sighed. "Not when he didn't dare leave his trademark."

Pellico still kept his Browning Hi-Power trained on Johnny. "I use 9 mm ammo. Most around here don't."

"You don't say."

Pico thought for a moment. "That would mean that Little Cock wanted me to take the heat."

"You'd take the heat anyway. You're the enforcement in this town. Little Squirt just wanted the Commission to jump to conclusions. That would take the heat off him long enough to set up a frame."

"I don't believe it."

"You think I'm imagining this bum shoulder?"

Pellico shook his head, looking stunned. He gnawed at that for a while, before saying, "The bullets were really there. Melody told me. Johnny here wouldn't have pulled a damn fool stunt like that on a *capo*, unless he was damn sure Little Squirt wouldn't be in any position to complain.''

Bolan grinned. ''You think so,'' he agreed.

Pellico's gun disappeared as smoothly as it had appeared.

''You two take the damnedest chances,'' he said.

''You'd think so,'' Bolan repeated. With his left hand, he slowly pushed down on his covers. The right hand was nestled across his chest, pointing the Beretta at The Picker.

The vulture who preyed on the young stared at the automatic for a long time.

''I might think so, but I'd be wrong. What's next?'' His voice shook.

Johnny stood up from where he'd been crouched, motionless. ''Next, help me get rid of these bodies.''

''You don't want Little Squirt to see them,'' Pellico agreed.

''Wrong,'' Bolan said from the bed. ''I want you two to leave them on Little Squirt's doorstep. It's time for me to send him a message.''

Both men sent surprised looks at Bolan. He couldn't give any explanations in front of The Picker.

''Just do it,'' he told them.

When Johnny was sure that Mack was watching him, he nudged Chop Chop's gun under the bed. Then he openly helped himself to the gun from the other corpse. The Picker and Johnny moved the bodies to the downstairs hall. Johnny didn't discover his bus was missing until he went out to bring it to the door. He searched the hall for his keys, while The Picker went to get his Lincoln.

The Picker drove the big car over the small lawn, right up to the front door. The less time they had the bodies on view the better. They were taking chances, but had to move the corpses before one of the hookers or actors returned to the house.

While Pellico brought the car, Johnny found another rug to roll around the corpse with the broken neck. They carried the two carpet rolls to the trunk. As soon as the second body was loaded, Pellico slammed the lid and got behind the wheel.

"What now, kid?" he asked, while he powered the Lincoln away from the house.

Johnny's attention was distracted by the sight of his bus. Twichen was driving it recklessly back to the place they'd just left. Johnny made a mental note to have a more forceful chat with Twichen later.

"I asked where we're going," Pellico snapped.

Johnny forgot about Twichen for the moment. He was almost glad the young actor would be there if Mack needed anything. Mack would be all right.

"We deliver the bodies to Schizzetto, as we were told," Johnny answered.

"You feel suicidal, or something?"

The Picker's knuckles were white on the steering wheel.

12

Johnny had Pellico park his Lincoln two hundred yards from Schizzetto's driveway. It was dark and a quarter moon hovered above the trees.

They carried the bodies through the damp bush to the iron fence. Then they returned to the car and put the rugs back in the trunk. The Picker turned the car around and left the motor running. Once more they trudged back to the bodies.

One at a time, they grabbed the corpses and swung them until they could heave them up onto the wrought-iron fence. As soon as the second body was draped over the iron pickets, Johnny and Pellico sprinted for the car. They could already hear Schizzetto's hard force reacting to the fence's alarm system.

"Let's move," Johnny said.

As soon as they were out of sight, Johnny said, "Now slow down. We don't want to be noticed. Then take the first right."

"What! Up the mountain. It's a dead end."

"I know. I've been up there."

"You going to get us in trouble, kid."

"I'm going to keep us alive."

Pellico sighed. "Okay. We'll do it your way. But if we're caught, I'm going to have the pleasure of shooting you before they get me."

Johnny ignored the threat. "There's room to pull the car out of sight between those two trees.

As soon as the car stopped, Johnny was out and moving farther up the mountain. After a moment's hesitation, Pellico followed him. Johnny led the way to a small clump of bush behind the Schizzetto estate. He'd watched the place from there earlier that day.

Floodlights now lit the yard, cutting through the light fog. A half-dozen hoods in guard uniforms held positions around the house, watching the perimeter. Another three struggled to pull the bodies off the iron pickets. Shouts echoed around the grounds.

"I didn't expect that size of hard force. Where'd they all come from?" Johnny asked.

Pellico gave Johnny another quizzical look. Johnny thought that it was becoming a habit. He knew it wasn't the right question to ask, but if the suitcase didn't show up he'd probably be going back for more weapons. He needed to know more about what he'd be up against. That was one of the reasons he had told Pellico to cut up behind the estate instead of making a run for it. The other reasons were now making themselves known.

Pellico opened his mouth to answer, but Johnny spoke first. "Look."

Although they couldn't see the cars for hedges and trees, the halos formed by headlights moving through the mist were easy to follow. Cars swept in from both ends of the winding road that went past Schizzetto's.

"Two corks in the bottle," Pellico observed. "How did you know they were there?"

"I wasn't sure," Johnny admitted, "but I saw houses at each end of the drive that looked too modest for the neighborhood. The crew wagons outside looked too showy to go with the houses. I thought it might be a possibility."

Again, Pellico's probing stare, barely discernible by the light of a quarter moon. "If you noticed that much, why are you asking me where the guards came from?"

"There weren't that many around this afternoon."

"Maybe they're changing guard. All I know is what I hear. I've only been there once, when my sales fell off. I don't want to go back again."

The Picker continued. "What they say is that Little Squirt has his own security service, set up legit downtown. But his own guards, who draw their pay through the service, use its uniforms and gun permits and live in two houses close by. I guess you spotted the houses."

"Time to leave," Johnny decided.

They went back to the car, pulled out of the trail and drove back toward Vancouver at a legal speed.

BOLAN WOKE the instant the door to his room opened. He still felt drained from the effort of dealing with The Picker and the two hoods in security uniforms who were hunting for Johnny. Bolan's first thoughts, before he focused on the person who entered the room, were for Johnny. Bolan knew he had to find strength before everything caved in on them.

Edgar Twichen came strolling into the room with such casual unconcern that Bolan knew he was up to something. The sense of threat cleared Bolan's head.

"Something I can do for you, Eddy?"

"Where's Johnny?"

"He's out for a while. Did you want anything in particular?

"Will he be back soon?" There was more concern in Twichen's voice than he'd intended to put there.

"In about an hour, I expect." Bolan was relieved that his sense of time was getting sharper. He didn't have to look at his watch to know how long he'd been sleeping.

"That isn't soon enough!" Twichen blurted.

"Soon enough for what?"

Twichen paused. Bolan could sense that he was about to lie. Before the porn actor could create his story, they heard the sound of the front door opening. Twichen's face lost its color.

"They mustn't find me here!" he gasped.

Before Bolan could probe further, Twichen was out the door and racing down the stairs at breakneck speed.

"What's the rush, Eddy." It was Megrims's voice.

"Oh! It's you."

Even from one flight up, Bolan could hear the vast relief in those three words. Twichen knew something and it frightened him. Bolan had to find a way to get Twichen back. Urgent questions required immediate answers.

"Melody, can you persuade Eddy to come up here and finish our conversation?" Bolan called out.

"Upstairs, Eddy," Bolan heard Megrims say.

"Can't. Got things to do."

Bolan pushed himself out of bed. He stood, but found his knees shaking. His shoulder ached only dully. Bolan pushed the pain from his mind and put all his concentration into walking.

"Eddy." There was a note of warning in Megrims's voice.

"Get out of my way. I've got no fight with you."

"You better just come upstairs."

"Out of my way, slut! Yeeow!" Twichen's voice went from anger to a howl of agony.

Fortunately, there was a handrail by the stairs down to the second floor. Bolan went to grasp it and found he'd instinctively picked up his Beretta 93-R when he left the bed. He transferred the gun to his left hand and started down the stairs, leaning heavily on the rail.

"What did you do that for? You could ruin a man, kneeing him like that." Twichen groaned with pain.

"If you don't like to get hurt, you shouldn't call people names." Megrims spoke in a mocking voice. "Besides, if it's only men that could get ruined that way, you've got nothing to worry about."

Bolan negotiated the last steps, which took a ninety-degree angle. He stood on the final step, swaying, surveying the second-floor hall. Twichen was on the floor in fetal position, both hands clasping his groin. Melody stood between him and the stairs to the first floor. Her face was as angry as it had been when she'd left Bolan several hours earlier.

Megrims turned her head and saw Bolan. At first, her angry look intensified, then it transformed itself into a smirk.

"You hot, or just advertising?" she asked.

Bolan suddenly realized he was naked. In his anxiety to catch Twichen, he had given no thought to what he was wearing, or not wearing. He smiled.

"Just waiting for you."

Her frown returned. "That's not funny."

"It wasn't meant to be. Can we discuss this later? Right now, we have things to talk over with Eddy." Bolan gestured with the Beretta. "Upstairs, Eddy."

"Can't walk," Twichen moaned.

"You want me in on this?" Megrims asked.

"Definitely."

Megrims turned to Twichen. "Crawl."

The word surprised Twichen to the extent that he forgot his pain and looked up at Melody. "What's that?"

"If you can't walk up those stairs, crawl. Better men than you have crawled up those steps." She turned to Bolan. "Can you make it back up?"

He took a deep breath and nodded. Then he stepped down the last step and to one side.

"Move," he told Twichen.

Twichen looked up and saw the Beretta staring him in the eye. Pulling himself to his feet, he hobbled to the stairs. He didn't crawl, but put only his right foot forward to each step, his torso doubled over until his face was within two feet of the stairs.

Melody brought up the rear, staying close to Bolan, positioning herself to support him if he started to fall. It was a slow climb, but they eventually made it to the bedroom. Bolan sat on the bed, perspiring freely. Twichen collapsed into a chair. Melody closed the door and leaned against it.

"What's this all about?" she asked.

"I think Eddy's expecting company. When you came to the door, he bolted. Said something about not letting them find him here."

She turned to look at Twichen, her face flushed with anger. "What's all this about?"

"Nothing. He's imagining things."

"Then you won't mind staying with us for a little while," Bolan told him.

The young actor couldn't hide the panic that flashed across his face. "I've got things to do." He tried to stand up.

Megrims took two strides into the room and shoved him back into the chair.

"You should never call yourself an actor, Eddy. You might as well wear a neon sign that says, 'I'm lying.'"

"Look. I've got to get out of here."

"Why?" Bolan demanded. "Who's coming? What for? Who sent them?"

"You're fishing."

"Like Melody told you, you're easy to read."

"Let me go!"

Bolan shook his head. "Whoever it is that comes will find that we're close buddies. And Melody knows that you're the only one I ever confide in."

Twichen turned white. "They'd kill me."

"Who?"

"I don't know. I didn't have anything to do with it. I followed Patricia back to the studio. She told Mr. Hanchovini that you're not who you say you are. He phoned someone called Salvatori and told him to get you and Johnny to talk and then check the story. Then I came back here. That's all I know, honest."

Megrims's face twisted with contempt. "You miserable little worm! First you follow people, then you come running back to see a sick man get beaten."

Twichen opened and closed his mouth a few times before he could answer. "I hate Johnny, and Corsaro's no better. They go out of their way to make me feel like an ass."

"So you wanted to see someone else work them over for you." Megrims's voice dripped scorn. "Did it ever occur to you that you're not going to bother growing up until you admit to yourself how small you really are?"

There was a moment's silence. Suddenly, for no apparent reason, Megrims blushed.

"You two better leave, now," Bolan told them.

"What about you?" Twichen asked.

"That trip downstairs convinced me that I won't have much luck running. But there's no reason either of you should be around. If things turn nasty, those boys won't leave any witnesses."

Twichen thought for a moment. "Why don't we phone the police?"

Bolan shook his head.

"What do they want you for?"

"Let's just say that if they held me for a few days, Schizzetto would have someone make sure that I never reached a courtroom."

"Schizzetto's Hanchovini's boss, isn't he?"

Bolan nodded.

"And I work for someone who'd have you killed, just like that?"

"You've always known that," Melody said in a strangled voice.

Before Twichen could answer, they heard the front door open.

"See who's on this floor. I'll watch the stairs and hall," a voice said.

Twichen and Megrims both paled. Megrims dashed from the room. Twichen stood up, facing the door, his fists clenched tightly.

"Get out and hide." Bolan commanded.

Twichen shook his head. "The film's not finished. They have money tied up in me. They may hurt me, but they won't kill me. Maybe, if there's a witness..." His voice trailed off.

"No one down here, Sal."

"Okay. Let's check out the second floor."

Bolan could hear feet on the stairs, then the sound of running feet in the second floor hallway.

"Hey! That was a broad. She went up to the third floor."

"Check out this floor first. I'll keep the traffic off the stairs."

The clatter of feet came down the hall and Melody burst back into the room with a suitcase in her hand. She ran to the bed and placed it beside Bolan, who simply looked at her.

"Hurry up," she told him. "It's the suitcase Johnny lost. I took it. It has guns in it."

Bolan continued to stare at her.

"I didn't know what was in it. I was angry because I felt so cheap. I knew it was for you, so when I got the opportunity, I hid it. I didn't know until later what was in it." She threw the case open. "Hurry," she urged him.

A voice from the doorway said, "Nobody move."

Bolan couldn't see the speaker, Melody stood between him and the doorway. Then the two men came into the room, one on each side of the bed.

"Move to one side. Do it slowly."

Melody looked at Bolan, who nodded. She slowly stepped sideways until she stood at the foot of the bed. One hood was four feet inside the door; the other crossed the room until he stood near the far wall. They both held Colt .45 automatics close to their sides. They were positioned to cover everyone in the room without being in each other's line of fire. Bolan knew professionals when he saw them. The one near the doorway moved forward until he could see what was in the case. He whistled low.

"I recognize those Swiss machine guns. I imagine Mr. Schizzetto will want to have a long talk with all of you."

"Is that where you're going to take us?" Twichen asked. His voice shook.

The hood who'd done all the speaking shook his head. "We'll phone him. He'll come here. We'd rather shoot you than parade you through the streets. Besides, there's someone named Johnny Gray. He doesn't seem to be here right now. We'll wait for him to show up, too."

The hood turned his attention to Bolan. "You must be C.C. You've got a lot of explaining to do."

Bolan sat on the edge of the bed, sweating. He was still naked.

13

"What's the problem?" Bolan asked.

"We don't know. It's none of our business. You just sit tight until we get someone else here."

The speaker turned to the other mobster. "Shorty, find a phone. Tell Mr. Hanchovini what we found. Let him get in touch with the Don. Ask him to send reinforcements. Then tell Tento to stay in the car and watch out for the Johnny Gray character. Let him get inside before moving in. After that, get back up here. We're taking no chances. Got that?"

Shorty nodded and hurried from the room. Salvatori had never let his attention wander from his prisoners.

"What are you going to do with us?" Twichen asked. His voice trembled.

"Shut up," Salvatori answered.

He studied Bolan for a while. "You're too close to those guns," he decided. "Move off the bed."

"I can't."

"If you don't, you'll get a bullet in the kneecap."

"I'm too weak," Bolan protested.

Salvatori worked the slide of the Colt.

Bolan started to roll to one side.

"Hold it! Bring your hands up one at a time. If you've got a gun in your hand it better get left behind in the bedding."

Bolan did as he was told. First, he leaned forward. Then his hands came into plain sight one at a time. He was forced to leave his Beretta lying in the crumpled bedclothes.

"Now, stand up."

Bolan rolled forward until most of his weight was over his feet. Then he slowly straightened his legs. He stood doubled over and swaying.

"Move from the bed to the chair," Salvatori commanded.

When Bolan tried to take a step, he collapsed to the floor.

Salvatori waved his automatic at Twichen. "Help him to the chair."

Twichen went over to Bolan and extended his hand, intending to take Bolan's good left arm. However, Bolan's right fist was already filled with the revolver Johnny had nudged under the bed. Twichen's eyes widened, then he gave a slight nod. An instant later, he whirled and made a low dive at the gunman's ankles.

The gunman swiped at Twichen's head with his weapon's barrel, but the blow never connected. A .357 Magnum slug blasted half his brain out of his head. The momentum of the swing caused the body to twist like a golfer's, then slowly sink to the floor.

The sound of the shot was still echoing in their ears when Shorty's voice came from downstairs. "Sal! Everything okay?"

Bolan managed a passable imitation of the dead man's voice. "Just had to teach the punk to stay still. No problem."

"You sure?"

"Come on up and see for yourself, Shorty."

"Forget it. Just don't let's have the neighbors phoning the cops."

Twichen picked himself up. He and Megrims hovered over Bolan, who was still on the floor beside the bed. He waved them away.

"My clothes," he told Melody. He turned to Twichen. "That was a brave move, Ed."

"Didn't know you had it in you," Melody said as she stepped over Salvatori's body on the way to the closet.

Twichen tried not to grin, but couldn't stop himself. Bolan watched him, waiting to see if his reaction would be overly modest or too cocky.

"T'weren't nothing," Twichen said with an affected Western drawl. "Any hero would have done it."

Bolan turned toward the bed, pulling himself to his feet while hiding a grin. Twichen's answer had a fine balance of self-congratulation and self-ridicule.

Melody produced his clothing. "Stay there. We'll dress you. You got to save your energy for making love and making war."

Bolan understood the statement for what it was—an apology and a question. Yeah, the kid felt badly that she'd taken the weapons and withheld them until it was too late.

The idea of having others dress him didn't appeal to Bolan, but he could not bring himself to refuse this vulnerable girl's peace offering.

"Thanks," Bolan said. He was still standing, but swayed slightly.

Bolan found himself in a strangely schizophrenic situation. One part of his mind was watching in amazement the efficiency with which Melody dressed him. It was as if she did daily drill in putting clothes on the wounded. The other part of his mind was tense, edgy, listening for the sound of feet on the stairs.

After Melody finished buttoning his shirt, Bolan sat on the edge of the bed and checked out the weapons in the suitcase. He slammed a fresh clip into his Beretta and tucked it away. Then he picked up one of the Swiss subguns, sniffed at it, then ejected the magazine and topped it up.

"What are we waiting for?" Twichen demanded.

"We can't get down those stairs without being wide open on the steps. Shorty'd cut our legs out from under us and then ask questions."

"So what do we do?"

"Wait until he comes up to us and we have the advantage, or until things start to happen and his attention's distracted."

"Isn't that leaving it too long?" Twichen asked.

Bolan nodded, eyes on the youngster.

"How about giving Melody and me each a gun?"

"Have you fired one before?"

Twichen hesitated before admitting, "No."

Bolan looked at Melody.

She shook her head. "I haven't, but I think Eddy and I have earned a piece of the action. We've made it our fight, too. We all win or lose together."

He thought for a moment.

"Okay," he agreed, "but hold your position and shoot where I tell you."

Bolan handed the Nambu to Megrims and showed her how to work the safety.

"Fire one shot at a time, otherwise it'll get away from you," he warned her.

He gave the revolver to Twichen. "Shoot low and remember this is going to kick harder than the gun I gave Melody."

Bolan put a spare magazine under his belt and picked up one of the Swiss submachine guns, then closed the suitcase and slid it under the bed. He led them down to the second floor. It was slow going, for they didn't want to announce their position to Shorty. They could hear him prowling the hall on the first floor.

He set the two young people by windows in the front of the house. Fortunately, the hookers who occupied the two rooms were already out on the street.

"When Johnny arrives, the hardman in that car is going to try to follow him into the house," Bolan whispered to his two recruits. "Shoot for the body, but don't shoot if there's anyone else in sight."

"What will you be doing?" Megrims whispered.

"The shooting will alert Johnny. It should also distract Shorty. That's when I'm going downstairs to have a chat with him."

"You'll never make it!" she exclaimed.

Bolan put a hand on her shoulder. "Trust me."

He turned and walked from the room, the MP-44 in his right fist. His easy stride cost him more energy than he cared to expend, but he had to maintain the confidence of the two young people. When he was in the hall, Bolan sat on the floor by the top of the stairs. He kept an eye on the stairs, but relaxed his muscles.

He'd done everything he could do to keep Twichen and Megrims alive, and to make sure Johnny didn't walk into a trap. He sat gripping the MP-44, breathing slowly and regularly, practicing the patience of the true warrior.

PATRICIA DANE DID NOT get to leave the studio right after Hanchovini's telephone call to Salvatori. Not anxious to return to his bookkeeping, Frankie Hanky decided to exercise his *droit du seigneur* as Dane's producer. He kept a chaise longue in his office for those times he wished to demonstrate his privileges of rank on one of his young serfs.

Dane, still willing to do anything easy to become a film star, made no objections. She divorced her mind from

Frankie Hanky's mechanical lovemaking by fantasizing that she was already a Hollywood queen and no longer had to make sleazy porn movies.

Afterward, Dane caught a taxi back to Jackson Street. Her mind was occupied with the usual dreams of stardom, but as she got closer to the Mob's home for wayward youth, she began to wonder if the man called Salvatori would still be there, questioning Gray and whoever that man was who called himself Johnny's brother.

As the cab pulled up to the curb, her thoughts were on Johnny and Corsaro. It was an unpleasant jolt to see Johnny step out of a Lincoln just ahead of her.

She slouched in the seat and fumbled with her wallet, willing Johnny to enter the house. She couldn't just stand there while that Salvatori person started asking all sorts of shrewd pointed questions.

She was fishing in her wallet for the correct change when a blur of motion caught the corner of her eye.

She looked up to see a man in a flashy suit cut behind the cab to follow Johnny toward the house. She stared, intrigued. She knew she was watching the Mob move in on Johnny. Now, maybe he'd learn to mind his own business.

The mobster was about fifteen feet from Johnny and about eight feet from the taxi when suddenly several shots erupted. One of them made a distinct plunking noise when it hit the hood of the taxi.

Johnny was the first to react. He glanced quickly at the front of the house, then dived and rolled to the front wall, beside the steps. He came up in a crouch, a revolver in his right fist.

The bullets continued to come from the second-floor windows. One plucked at the mobster's suit jacket. He raised his weapon, holding it in both hands, sighting it on one of the windows.

Johnny yelled, "Throw down your gun."

The hood in the street paused, then lowered his sights to take care of Johnny. Johnny's revolver spoke first. His bullet caught the mobster in the knee. The man spun and pitched forward, falling toward the taxi. His head intersected the path of a bullet from the upstairs window. Dane had a close-up view as the second bullet punched the mobster forward, bits of face and brain splattering on the fender. Then the front of the head struck, leaving a dark smear as it sank to the ground.

"Shit!" the taxi driver exclaimed.

The sudden action had frozen him in his seat, but the sight of the faceless corpse smearing his fender, jolted him into action. He jammed the shift into drive and floored the accelerator.

Johnny leaped onto the front steps and threw the door open. He paused to peer around the doorjamb then stepped inside. There was a sudden fusillade and Johnny pitched forward.

Dane's stomach threatened to rise through her chest and crush her lungs. She had seen Johnny fall. If Corsaro were still alive, she might well be the next faceless corpse. That would not happen to her, no matter who had to die. She could see no way of guaranteeing her own survival, short of having the Mafia finish the bloody job.

She pulled herself erect and told the driver, "Let me out at the first pay phone."

"You going to call the cops?"

"Someone has to."

"I just wasn't there, lady. I just wasn't."

"I'll keep it anonymous."

The driver pulled to a stop by a restaurant. They could see the pay phone through the front window. Forgetting her resolution not to tip the driver, Dane handed him a ten and stepped onto the curb.

It wasn't the police Dane telephoned from the restaurant; it was the studio. There was no answer. She looked in the telephone book, but no Hanchovini was listed.

It took a few minutes' thought, but she finally remembered the name of Frankie Hanky's boss. She'd heard it around the house only recently. Schizzetto was listed. She put in her coin and dialed.

"Schizzetto residence," a cultured male voice answered.

"I must speak to Mr. Schizzetto. It's urgent. One of his business associates has just had an overdose of lead."

There was a pause on the other end, then the voice asked in the same matter-of-fact tones, "You mean someone's been shot?"

"Yes."

"Just a moment." The mouth at the other end of the line didn't back off from the telephone before yelling, "Boss, some broad on the phone. Something about someone getting shot. She seems to think you should be told about it."

Dane jerked the receiver away from her ear and held it there until a gruff voice said, "Yeah?"

"I'm Patricia Dane."

"So?"

"I act at Lion's Gate Productions."

"Big deal."

"This evening I told Mr. Hanchovini that there was something strange about Corsaro Cancellari and Johnny Gray. They're staying at the house on Jackson Street."

"Never heard of 'em."

Dane took a deep breath and plowed ahead. "So he told someone called Salvatori to take someone else and go check them out."

"Good for Frankie."

"I live at that house. I was just getting back there and almost walked into a gunfight. Johnny Gray was killed, but so was the...ahh...person who was left outside to take care of him. Salvatori and whoever was inside must have been killed, because the gunshots came from inside.

"I don't know what happened there, but I'm trying to contact Mr. Hanchovini. He's no longer at the studio and I don't know how to reach him. So, I figured I should call you."

The gruff voice on the other end of the phone had stopped making rude interruptions. When Dane finished there was a pause before it asked, "Why call me?"

"Because you're Mr. Hanchovini's boss."

"Who said?"

"I think it was Mr. Cancellari, at the house." Dane wasn't sure who it was, but now that she was committed to getting those two out of her life, she'd better finish the job.

"And Frankie sent Salvatori to the house?"

"I was there when he make the call."

"Okay. I'll send a crew to take care of the mess. You'd better stay away from there. You get a taxi up here so I can thank you. You got that?"

"I'll be there as soon as I can," she promised.

Schizzetto made sure she had the address right, then hung up.

Dane walked out of the restaurant smiling. All her troubles would be over very soon.

14

Johnny Bolan stood on the curb and watched The Picker's Lincoln drive away. His mind was preoccupied with the missing suitcase. It had been a while since Johnny had been with the U.S. Marines in Beirut. There, every shadow might hold a fanatic with an automatic weapon and the American who didn't stay constantly alert didn't stay alive.

But it takes only a few years away from danger for high-level alertness to relax. So Johnny's first hint of trouble was the sudden burst of single-shot gunfire from two upstairs windows. Once the firing began, his combat reactions took over.

A long dive, a tuck and short roll brought him to the base of the wall, out of the sniper's range. Only after he was crouched, holding the dead guard's revolver, did Johnny realize the bullets weren't meant for him. The only logical alternative was that they were meant for someone behind him. That someone must have been stalking him.

A guy was standing in the street, having a regular shoot-out with the two at the windows. The bullets coming from the upstairs windows were too high, a sign of inexperienced gunmen. Johnny decided he'd better take care of the one in the street before trying to enter the house. But he wasn't absolutely sure of the players.

"Drop your gun," Johnny yelled.

The gunman responded by lowering his sights to take out Johnny. No further identification needed. He blasted the man's right knee before he could shoot. One of the weapons upstairs was getting better range: the gunman fell into the path of a bullet.

Johnny's chief concern was Mack. There were probably more scum inside. And who had been firing from the window? Johnny knew he had to get to his brother.

Johnny jumped to the front stoop and threw the door open, staying to one side. No bullets came flying out to meet him. He moved cautiously inside. The lights were out, making it difficult to see.

Suddenly a figure leaned into the hall from the front room, aiming something at Johnny. He threw himself flat just as a burst of automatic fire from the stairs knocked the gunman back into the front room.

"Johnny, you okay?" It was Mack's voice.

Relief surged through the ex-Marine's veins. He hadn't realized how tense he was until he heard his brother's voice. "Yeah. What's happening?"

Bolan picked his way unsteadily from his position halfway down the stairs. He lowered himself until he was sitting on the third step from the bottom. There was enough light from the street that Johnny could tell Mack was carrying one of the Swiss SMGs

"You found the guns?"

"Later. Get the suitcase. It's under the bed. Grab anything with your identity on it. Collect Megrims and Twichen from the second floor. We have less than two minutes to get out of here."

Johnny's Marine training took over again. He ran to obey, and they were all in Johnny's van and pulling away from the curb in just over one minute. Already the first approaching siren could be heard.

"What about Patricia?" Johnny asked as he drove through the downtown evening traffic.

"She hasn't returned from a late-night visit to the studio," Bolan told him.

Twichen started to fill in all the details, apologizing for borrowing the van.

Johnny interrupted him. "Where are we going? I think we should ditch this vehicle. Then there's Patricia. How are we going to prevent her from walking right into the arms of the police, providing the Mob lets her go? And what do we do if the Mob doesn't let her go?"

"First, let's get off the street in case someone saw us pull away in this," Bolan said. "Any suggestions where?"

"I think I know a good spot," Melody said, "but it'll only be good for a couple of days."

Everyone paused, waiting for her to continue.

"Shirley Queen used to live with us on Jackson Street. She has enough regulars that she moved into her own apartment a few weeks ago. She'll be on the street, but I've got a key to her apartment. Best of all, an underground parking space comes with the apartment and she has no car."

"Can we trust her?" Johnny asked.

"Definitely. She was suckered into this racket, just like I was. In her case, the money's a gambling debt. She's one of the few Mafia-owned hookers I know who hasn't got a habit. Anyway, she has no love for her present owners."

"What's the catch?" Bolan asked.

"What do you mean?"

"You said the location would be good only for a couple of days. That means there's some form of risk. What is it?"

"She isn't as...ah...easily handled as I was. The Picker, or one of his men looks in on her fairly frequently."

Bolan noticed the word "was" and felt pleased. His judgment told him not to make an issue of it.

"Let's go," he said.

He leaned back in the seat and felt his wounded shoulder. It had begun to swell.

The address Megrims gave Johnny turned out to be a new apartment tower in the west end. Melody's key was all that was needed to raise the door to the parking area under the building.

The apartment was on the twentieth floor, and had two bedrooms and a view of Coal Harbour. It was crowded with cheap, secondhand furniture. However, there was food in the efficiency kitchen, and an arborite-and-chrome table with matching chairs where they could sit and talk while they ate. Johnny and Melody prepared a meal of canned spaghetti and peanut butter sandwiches.

"It was this or beans and corn flakes," Johnny explained. "Our hostess seems to have limited culinary skills."

As they sat down to the table, Bolan told Megrims and Twichen, "I'll take those handguns back."

Megrims pulled the Nambu from her purse and handed it to him, butt first.

"What the hell for?" Twichen objected. "We may not be out of trouble yet."

"You might as well," Johnny told him. "It's empty."

"How do you know?"

"You fired your six bullets."

Twichen pulled the gun from under his shirt and dropped it on the table. He was too angry to speak.

"By the way, thank you for saving my life," Johnny told him.

That caused Twichen to brighten, but all he said was, "You're not welcome."

Bolan finished his dinner, yawning several times before scooping up the last forkful. He refused coffee and wandered over to a worn sofa, where he flopped down and was asleep almost immediately.

Johnny helped Megrims with the dishes, picked up the suitcase and set it upright beside the sofa. Then he found a pillow and a blanket and curled up to sleep on the floor. The suitcase was safe between himself and Mack.

Twichen slouched around for a while, then went into one of the bedrooms. Megrims stepped around Johnny, who opened one eye but didn't stir. She ran her hands over Bolan's shoulder. It was hard and hot.

She stepped back and whispered to Johnny, "I don't like that shoulder."

"I noticed it was bothering him. Let him sleep, we'll have to do something in the morning."

She nodded. She shifted a fairly comfortable chair to the hall and settled down to snooze and wait for her friend, Shirley, to return.

Bolan woke about nine the next morning. He felt more rested than he had for some time, but his shoulder was hot and swollen. He opened his eyes, not surprised to find he was the last one up.

When Melody saw that he was awake, she brought him a cup of coffee.

"Shirley didn't get in until four," Melody told him. "She says welcome. She's still asleep. The rest of us are up and we're worried about Patricia."

Bolan could see Johnny and Twichen sipping coffee at the table. Empty breakfast dishes were pushed away from the places. He couldn't believe he'd slept through that much activity.

"What's wrong with Patricia?"

"According to the girls at Jackson Street, she never showed up last night. The last time anyone saw her was when Eddy followed her to the studio. When she's working, she usually gets lots of sleep."

Bolan took a sip of coffee, then sighed. "We're going to the studio," he decided.

"When?"

"Right away. The longer we wait, the less chance she has."

"Breakfast first."

Bolan thought for two seconds. "Only if it's fast. I'll brief the rest of you while I eat."

RUDOLFO SCHIZZETTO looked up from his breakfast of sausages and eggs to scowl at Patricia Dane.

"What's the matter," he snapped. "My hospitality ain't good enough for you? I treat you good and you try to leave."

Dane stood before him, her arms held by two burly thugs in guard uniforms. She could smell the sausage—just barely—through the stench of the unwashed guards. The smells and the fear were causing her stomach to knot.

"I've got a film to make," she told the gangland boss. "I thought you'd want me to go to work."

"You thought," he thundered. "Who the hell told you to think? While you're here, you do as I say."

Dane's temper flared. "You've got no right to hold me prisoner. When Frankie finds out you're not going to let me go to the studio, he'll be furious."

"Frankie! You got no manners? Mr. Hanchovini to you."

He turned to his guards. "Teach the slut some manners. Throw her in her room and put someone on the door. Then tell the gate that Mr. Hanchovini should be arriving soon. I want to see him right away."

"Fr...Mr. Hanchovini's coming here?" Dane asked.

"I didn't speak to you. Teach her manners. Teach her good," Schizzetto thundered. As they started to turn, he added, "No damage. She's got enough looks to be worth something."

It was only when she heard the part about no damage, that the young porn actress understood what "teach her manners" meant. She moaned and her knees refused to support her weight.

Dane was dragged from the dining room to the shooting gallery. It was soundproof. An excellent place for playing twenty questions and giving lessons in Mob etiquette.

Schizzetto was just sopping the last egg yolk from his plate when Frankie Hanchovini was escorted into his presence. The Don waved for the guards to go, but he didn't offer his lieutenant a chair, nor coffee. An ominous sign that didn't escape Hanchovini's attention.

"What the hell's happening?" the Don demanded.

"In what way?"

"'In what way?'" Schizzetto mimicked. "I got some stupid twit on the telephone last night. She's one of your kiddy porn idiots. First of all, she knows that I'm connected to the studio. You get paid to front that and you get paid good. Yet, this broad knows I'm behind it."

"No one heard it from me," Hanchovini answered firmly. He was nervous, but too shrewd to let it show.

"Then she tells me that you had Sal take a couple of boys over to the house to talk to some guy named Corsaro and another named Johnny Gray. She tells me Salvatori and the boys got wasted. I sent a couple of crew wagons around, but the joint's crawling with police and the meat wagon's there."

"Shit! That's why I didn't hear back from him." Frankie Hanky couldn't keep the shock out of his voice.

"Who are they and what the hell were they doing there?"

"C.C., that's Corsaro Cancellari, is a hotshot from the head shed. He claimed we owed him for cleaning up in San Francisco, after we left there. He knew the right names and facts. He had a shoulder wound. I let him lay over for a while. He seemed clean."

"Seemed clean! He could be a Mountie, anybody."

Frankie took the insults. He had no choice. Besides, what were a few insults when a man's life was a stake? He simply stood, ashen faced, until Little Squirt's tirade ran down and then continued with his story.

"Anyhow, when the Dane broad came to me last night and said something was fishy, I phoned The Picker right away. He wasn't there so I asked Salvatori to check him and this Gray guy out thoroughly. I made a mistake, but C.C.'s wounded and I didn't think the young punk could make any trouble."

"Someone sure as hell made trouble. We have one hell of a mess on our hands."

"Where's Dane, now? What's she say?"

"She's probably still downstairs getting a lesson in manners. Dumb broad tried to walk out of here without permission."

"Stop it right away. You're throwing away five-hundred big ones."

"What are you talking about?"

"We've just about wrapped up the biggest hardcore production yet. It's worth millions to us and we have $500,000 invested in it. If she's badly disfigured, we'll have to re-shoot."

"Louis!" Little Squirt shouted.

Louis was the Don's new head cock. He was a huge man and wore an AutoMag in a shoulder holster. The stainless-steel cannon was well proportioned to his size. When Schizzetto shouted, Louis nearly flew into the room.

"Yeah, boss."

"Go find where they're working over that broad and have her brought back here, pronto."

"Yes, sir."

Schizzetto turned to glare at Frankie Hanky. "We can't just let her walk. Her mouth's too big."

"You've always trusted my judgment before."

"You never messed up as bad as this C.C. thing."

"Look, boss. She's a snap to handle. All we do is tell her that we've got her a Hollywood part. We tell her that before we release her, she's got to do this film for us and one more. That the second one is so rush she has to stay at the studio.

"That way we get to finish our big porn pic. Then we feature her in a fast snuff film. She doesn't talk anymore and our profit goes up."

"How do you get her to do a snuff film? Not even that broad's stupid enough to do a pic where she gets tortured to death."

"Hell, she's too dumb to know what a snuff film is. We'll shoot all the other scenes, just like another porn job, check the negs and then snuff her."

"She'll buy that?" Little Squirt was skeptical.

"Just watch," Frankie assured him as Louis brought Dane in.

Frankie immediately went to Dane and put his arm around her. "You okay, Miss Dane?"

She was bruised, bawling, and too terrified to answer.

"Look," Frankie told her, "everyone here made a mistake. You shouldn't have bothered the boss. He's a very busy man. At least you should have let him know who you were."

Her look was one of skepticism.

"Tell her, Mr. Schizzetto."

Little Squirt said in a bored voice, "That's right. I was sure you were putting me on. I didn't know you're the one who's going to go on to Hollywood."

The magic word rivetted her attention. "Hollywood?"

"Sure," Frankie told her. "You think you're working for bums who don't keep their word? I arranged a part for you last night. Then I get over here and you're giving Mr. Schizzetto trouble. That wasn't very smart, was it?"

"A part!"

"It ain't the lead. You'll be the supporting actress, but it's a start."

"When do I audition?"

"Audition? Don't be silly. The producer's already seen you in two of the pics you did for me. He was glad to promise you the part."

Dane looked around, willing herself to believe the greatest news she'd ever heard. Frankie didn't give her time to figure things out.

"We got to do something about those bruises. I'll cancel shooting today, but we got to go tomorrow, if you're going to finish this picture, and do us one more before you go. I guess the next one will be your last for Lion's Gate Productions. I'll miss you."

"Really?" The extra work and the supporting role instead of leading role were beginning to convince her.

"I promise that the film after this one will be your last for Lion's Gate."

Schizzetto gave a snort of laughter, but managed to get himself back under control.

"Will you stay here until tomorrow? I'll send a car for you then. In the meantime, we'll have a doctor look at those bruises. Makeup will help, but we'll have to get the swelling down."

"I recommend a Dr. Volta," Dane said. "She's the one who took the bullets out of C.C.'s shoulder."

"Is she now?" Little Squirt mused.

"Now, apologize to Mr. Schizzetto and we'll get you fixed up."

"I'm sorry, Mr. Schizzetto," Dane said. She didn't sound sorry; she sounded full of dreams for the future.

Schizzetto nodded absentmindedly. As soon as Frankie took Dane out of the room, the Mafia boss turned to Louis.

"I want two crews of men on this Dr. Volta at all times. If that C.C. used her once, he may go back to her."

Louis snatched up the telephone and started issuing orders.

When he was through, Schizzetto took the phone and got through to The Picker.

"I need extra men," he told the enforcer. "I want them farther down the mountain than the barracks my troops use. If there's trouble here, I want you to come up behind my boys as a second wave. You got that?"

"Sure, Mr. Schizzetto. You expecting trouble?"

"Just an insurance policy," he told Pellico. "When you have them in position, establish communications with Louis." He hung up without waiting for an answer. It didn't matter. No one said "no" to Rudolfo Schizzetto.

"No matter which way that bastard jumps, we've got him," Little Squirt told his new security chief.

15

Mack Bolan, Johnny, Megrims and Twichen sat in the Volkswagen bus down the street from Lion's Gate Productions.

"Hanchovini's car isn't in his parking spot," Twichen said. "Are you going in to look for Patricia before he gets here?"

Bolan shook his head. "If she's not there, we'll want to ask him some questions. We wait."

"But anything could be happening to her in the meantime," Melody protested.

"Anything could have happened to her by now," Bolan answered. "We wait because it gives us the best chance of finding her alive."

Melody shifted uncomfortably. She was sitting at the wheel of the bus. "I'm supposed to just sit here, while you macho types go roaring around the studio playing cops and robbers?"

"You got it," Johnny told her. "How else would you have it?"

"Ed's going in with you, because he knows the layout. I guess I'd rather C.C. stayed here. He's still too weak for this type of thing."

"The shoulder's too stiff for wheeling our getaway transportation, but I still have a better chance than you of keeping the gunplay to a minimum,'' Bolan told her. "I'm afraid you have the hard job, waiting.''

"Just so you realize it,'' she sniffed.

"What about a gun for me?'' Twichen asked for the third time.

"Not until you've had more practice.''

Twichen had no reply, so he lapsed into a moody silence. The rest felt disinclined to talk further. They sat in uneasy quiet, each with his own thoughts.

At 10:36 A.M., Twichen said, "He's pulling into his parking spot, now.''

"Where will he go first?'' Bolan asked.

"It isn't always the same; probably his office.''

"We'll follow him in. Stay close enough to see where he's going, but far enough back that he doesn't notice us before we move in,'' Bolan said.

The three men climbed out of the Volkswagen and stretched their cramped limbs. Johnny carried the used suitcase. He had the Nambu in his belt. It had eight rounds in the box clip and another in the chamber. The lack of spare clips had forced him to carry some loose rounds in his sports coat pocket. The other jacket pocket held spare magazines for the two MP-44s in the suitcase.

Bolan had the silenced Beretta 93-R in its snap-away shoulder rig. It was concealed by a light Windbreaker Megrims had purchased for him. In the jacket's pockets was a supply of spare clips for both the Beretta and the Swiss subguns.

They arrived in the foyer just as the elevator doors were closing on Frankie Hanky. At Bolan's signal, they waited for the building's only elevator to return to the ground floor for them.

"His office is on the fifth, yet he got off at the third floor. That means he's going to the sound stage,'' Twichen said.

"Was Dane supposed to be on set today?" Bolan asked.

"Both of us were."

"Then we'll go to the sound stage," Bolan decided. "There's a chance they'll try to get the film finished. The Mob hates to lose money on any investment. They don't seem to understand cutting losses. That may keep Dane alive and in reasonable health, but don't count on it."

Twichen shivered.

They stepped off the elevator into a drab gray hall that ran the width of the building to fire stairs on either side. Office doors opened from one side of the hall. The other side was featureless except for the opening of another hall which ran toward the back of the building from beside the elevator.

"Directors' and casting offices across the front. Going toward the back of the building, it's sound stage on the right, dressing rooms, wardrobe and makeup on the left," Twichen explained.

"Where would Hanchovini most likely go?" Johnny asked.

Twichen shrugged.

"If you're missing, and Dane as well, the shooting schedule will be off. Who'd he talk to about that?" Bolan wanted to know.

"He and the director would be on the set."

"Let's go."

They walked a hundred feet toward the back of the building before coming to a door with a red light on one side and a green light on the other. The green light was on, indicating that they weren't shooting at the moment.

"I didn't expect anything this professional," Johnny said.

"Videotape," Twichen answered.

"How's that?"

"Since video machines became so cheap, anyone can make a videotape of people screwing. The professionals have had to improve their product to keep the market. It isn't Hollywood, but it gets more professional all the time. Especially the sort of thing Patricia and I do.

"There's big money for kiddy porn. A lot of weirdos out there want to see children doing it. Dane and I can be made to look very young. As soon as we start looking over thirteen we won't be worth shit. Most of our fellow actors are fourteen and under, except the old ones. Every now and then, one of us has to make out with someone who looks ancient." Twichen's voice was as matter-of-fact as a tour guide's as he led them through the double sound doors.

"Now and then we have to do a film for the schools. That's what the police, etcetera, think we do all the time," Twichen added.

He would have continued with his guided tour, but Bolan interrupted, "Stay behind us. We expect trouble."

They emerged into a room that was two stories high. Overhead, grips worked on catwalks, shifting lighting. There was a set of a bedroom at one end of the studio. It was as Melody had described. The bed and furnishings were all fifty percent larger than life, dwarfing the naked girl who sat there propped against the huge pillows.

A cinematographer was using a spot meter to take light readings. Periodically he'd take his eye from the meter and direct the placement of another light. Sound technicians were busy fiddling with microphones and recording levels. In one corner, Frankie Hanky was having a low-voiced conversation with a six-foot-six bean pole with blond hair.

"That's Lester Knight, the director," Twichen informed Bolan without prompting. "He does all the films here, but there are two assistants to take care of most of the scenes. Knight usually directs the kinky sex and violence stuff himself. The girl on the bed's called Panda something. She lies around for all the setups. She's been no good on screen since she lost sixty percent of her skin doing a whip flick."

When he looked, Bolan could see that what he thought were irregularities in the lighting were really massive amounts of scar tissue. Even the breasts were grossly deformed. The corners of Bolan's jaws turned white as the muscles tensed.

He turned to Johnny. "Forget the finesse. It's time for the artillery."

Johnny undid the latches, handed Bolan an MP-44, then set the suitcase by the door where he could pick it up on the way out. Bolan took the subgun and walked over to where two grips were pulling on two large lights on wheeled dollies.

"Turn them on and hold them focused on Hanchovini," Bolan told them.

"Are you nuts?" one began.

Bolan thrust the muzzle of the gun under his chin.

"If you had any brains, I wonder how far they'd spread," Bolan mused.

The other grip hastened to obey orders. The one with the gun under his chin started to say something else. Then he looked into the remorseless blue of Bolan's eyes and hastened to do as he was told. Suddenly two strong spots stabbed out, pinning Frankie Hanky and the director in their concentrated glare. He swung around, scowling.

"There's a fire alarm by the door," Bolan told the grips. "If you pull it before you go, I won't shoot. But you'd better keep going right out of the building and avoid the stampede. You got that?"

"Yes, sir," they both answered at once and took off, running.

"What the hell's going on?" Frankie thundered, squinting to see what was happening behind the lights.

Bolan sent a short burst through overhead lights, raining glass down on the cameramen.

"Everyone out except Hanchovini and Knight."

Then the alarms started to sound, starting a general stampede toward the door. The producer and director of Mafia porn turned to run, too, but found themselves staring into the barrel of Johnny's MP-44. Johnny gestured that they should walk toward the klieg lights. Shielding their eyes with their hands, they did so. Johnny kept pace to one side, out of Mack's line of fire. From the side it wasn't necessary to look into the lights to keep the jackals covered.

"Who the hell's that?" the mobster demanded.

Bolan ignored the question. "Where's Dane?"

"How the hell should I know? She ain't here." Hanchovini had to shout over the sound of the alarm.

Bolan's voice was the voice of doom. "If you don't know where she is, this picture's a bust. And if this investment's a washout, you are, too."

"Is that you, C.C.?"

"The same. Now, is this investment washed out or isn't it?"

"Who sent you?"

"If you don't have a business, you don't need a director," Bolan answered.

The door burst open and four thugs came pouring in. Their drab-green uniforms, each complete with a holstered Colt New Frontier, were starting to look like standard issue for Vancouver thugs. This quartet was a matched set for the guards at Schizzetto's. Three of them managed to fire wild shots at Bolan before Johnny turned and stitched a figure eight through all four for a perfect strike.

Knight leaped on Johnny's back. Bolan put a single bullet through the smut director's brain.

"See," he told Hanchovini, "you don't need him. You're bankrupt."

"She's alive," Frankie screamed. "She's at Little Squirt's. She's just had a little accident, but she'll be here tomorrow."

"What sort of an accident?"

"Little Squirt had her worked over some, but I stopped him. I knew we had to finish the movie and pay off on the investment. You tell the bosses. Their money's safe."

"Torch the place, Frankie."

"What!"

"Those backdrops should start a good bonfire. Do it," Bolan barked.

Hanchovini hesitated. Bolan put a bullet through the toe of his shoes. The mobster who had girls flayed for his movies screamed. He quickly got out his lighter and lit it, then hobbled toward the set.

While the Bolan brothers watched Frankie Hanky carry the torch, Twichen moved quietly to the closest dead guard. He picked up a fallen revolver and put it in his belt, under his shirt.

Frankie bent toward the set with his back to Bolan and Johnny. He dropped the lighter and snatched at the big AutoMag under his jacket. A single shot went through the bridge of his nose to make a large splash in his brain. He collapsed without firing a shot.

Bolan moved forward and kicked the still-burning lighter into the painted backdrop. It caught immediately. Stacked behind the set were a selection of other painted backdrops. When the flames grew, the fire would easily ignite the unused sets and furnishings.

Bolan bent to pick up the AutoMag. It felt good to have one in his hand again. Then he followed Twichen and Gray out the door. In the hall, Bolan shoved the AutoMag into his belt and pulled his Windbreaker over it. He handed the MP-44 to Johnny, who stored both subguns in the suitcase. The three of them walked quickly to the stairs and joined the press of people escaping the screaming fire alarm.

They were on the landing at the second floor level when a man charged out and slammed into Bolan, knocking him hard against the wall. An explosion of pain consumed Bolan's shoulder, but he staggered, pulled himself upright and kept going. The panicked rabbit hadn't noticed the collision.

The three were just part of the crowd leaving the building. Firetrucks had begun to arrive. Wisps of smoke were beginning to rise from one side of Lion's Gate Productions. They walked calmly back to the bus.

"He's been shot again in the same shoulder!" Melody gasped as Bolan climbed into the van.

That was the first time Bolan realized that his shoulder was bleeding. He had deliberately kept his mind off it in order to handle the pain.

"I got bumped. The wound opened up again," Bolan told her.

Megrims put the vehicle in motion and drove in smooth, efficient haste.

"Fortunately, we're not too far from Dr. Volta's office. You have to get that tended."

Bolan was examining the heavy seepage of foul-looking blood.

"I guess that's safest," he said.

16

Dr. Eleonora Volta's office was in a new yellow brick building in downtown Vancouver that contained the largest collection of doctors, dentists and other practitioners of the healing arts on the West Coast.

Nino Rossini was bored out of his mind. He had been sitting in the front seat of the Caddy Seville since 8:30, listening to Art Rocca, the wheelman, pop his bubble gum. It was now 11:30. If he had to put up with another three hours of it, he'd kill the punk himself.

In the back seat, Vito Baccliono continued his litany of complaint to Luigi Mosca, who had no choice but to listen.

"This is stupid! Four of us sit here all day with four more in the car at the other door. Volta ain't going nowhere until she sees her patients. Of all the stupid—"

"I got an idea," Nino interrupted.

"Yeah?" Vito lit up. He was finally getting through to someone.

"Luigi, Art and I will sit here, like stupids. You grab a cab back to North Van and tell Little Squirt how stupid this is."

Luigi and Art burst into fits of laughter. All 280 pounds of Vito turned dynamite red.

"Why, you..." Vito began.

Nino was already turning in his seat. His hazel eyes bored into the giant's black ones.

"Yes?" Nino prompted.

"Nothin'." Vito leaned back and immersed himself in sullen silence.

The other two swallowed their laughter and stared straight ahead. Nino was not only the crew boss, but also someone to be handled with the same respect one handled a vial of nitroglycerine.

Nino faced front and peered through the windshield. Then he flicked an imaginary piece of lint from his dark-blue pinstriped suit and said in a calm voice, "I'll bet that's one of them."

"I think that's blood on the shoulder of his jacket," Art exclaimed. "It's probably the Cancellari guy. I wonder where Gray is."

Nino's voice picked up tempo, crackling with decisiveness. "Vito, Luigi follow him. If he goes into that Volta broad's office, Vito is to watch the door, and Luigi, you come back and get the rest of us."

While the two in the back seat jumped to obey, Nino picked up the microphone of the car's CB.

"This is Lot. Do we have the doorman there?"

The reply came right back. "Doorman's listening. What have you got?"

"A probable going up. Stand by."

"What the hell do you think we've been doing all along?" the doorman replied.

Nino was hanging the microphone back in the cradle when Rocca exclaimed, "There's Gray. Over there."

He pointed to a young man wearing horn-rimmed glasses who was climbing out of a sky-blue Volkswagen bus. Nino had to admit Rocca was probably right. Gray, if that was who is was, walked right by the Caddy without giving it a glance, and entered the building. He carried a cheap suitcase that Nino wouldn't have used to put out garbage.

"Follow him," Nino told Art. "If he goes to Volta's, stay with Vito until we get there. If he heads somewhere else, use your shiv."

A look of unholy glee spread over the young hood's face as he sprang from the car. Telling Rocca to use his knife was like promising a kid an entire gallon of ice cream. Nino picked up the microphone to keep the other car informed, hoping that Art would stop with one corpse and not carve up bystanders in order to prolong his fun.

MELODY PARKED THE VAN and went up to the office alone. Ten minutes later, she was back.

"Dr. Volta is willing to take an emergency ahead of her regular patients. Besides, there's only one waiting at the moment. Just remember, you've had an accident at work," Melody told Bolan.

"Ed and I will gas up this buggy and meet you back here," Johnny told them.

Bolan followed Melody into the building and up to the eighteenth floor. Several people on the elevator stared at his Windbreaker with its growing stain of dark red. Yeah, inconspicuous he wasn't. If he was to move around freely, he needed the shoulder treated and clean clothing.

Melody had been thinking the same thing. She stopped outside the office and told Bolan, "You go on in. Dr. Volta's expecting you. Stay here until I get back. I'll bring you a fresh shirt and jacket."

"Thanks."

She nodded and left. At the elevators, she passed a small man who had come up on the elevator with them. He was looking lost. When the next elevator arrived, a giant of a man stepped off, giving her a quizzical look as he did so. Megrims's mind was on the need to hurry. She paid him no attention.

Bolan entered the office. There was no one there but a redheaded receptionist. She gave Bolan a wide smile.

"Dr. Volta is with a patient, Mr. Cancellari. She'll be with you in less than five minutes."

Bolan was about to sit down, when a door to an inner office opened and Volta emerged, speaking soothingly to a woman of about fifty.

"Check into the hospital Tuesday night," she told the patient. "I'll be there early Wednesday to talk to you. It's a minor operation. You have nothing to worry about, Mrs. Lemon."

The woman gave her a smile of gratitude as she headed for the door of the office.

Dr. Volta smiled at Bolan and ushered him into her private office, indicating that he should sit up on an examining table. Without saying anything, she helped him remove his jacket. When she saw the Beretta in the shoulder rig, she shook her head and said, "We'll slide this under the jacket. No use upsetting my nurse, if I have to call her in." Then she helped him off with the blood-soaked shirt and dropped it into a scrub sink. She examined the wound closely, occasionally probing tender areas, mopping up the seepage with a small towel.

"Has there been swelling recently?" she asked.

"Yes."

"And the wounded shoulder has recently been squeezed or struck?"

"I stumbled and knocked into a wall."

"Well, I'll have to go back into that wound and find the source of the infection, but this seepage is actually going to speed up the healing. I imagine you already have more freedom of movement in your shoulder than you had before you struck it."

Bolan flexed his shoulder. "Yeah. It's freer."

"I'm going to freeze the shoulder. The needles will hurt. I'll have to put them right into tender areas. After that, you'll feel what I'm doing, but no pain."

"Go ahead," he told her.

She injected local anesthetic in several areas. Then she picked up a scalpel, her hands seeming to take on a life of their own. They sterilized the area, enlarged one of the previous incisions and probed the area with small, sharp spoons. Soon the blood from the area was clear and red. She packed the area with antibiotic and closed the wound.

"Healing should be much faster, now," she told him as she tied the final stitch. As Dr. Volta was bandaging the shoulder, the door burst open and two thugs waving Mac 10s exploded into the room.

"Okay, Doc. We'll take care of your patient now." The goon spoke with a pronounced New York accent.

The two spread into the examining room. Bolan was aware of the Beretta beside him, under his jacket. But even if he could grab it, he couldn't get a clear shot at both jackals. He started to raise his arms.

"Keep your hands still!" she commanded him. "I'm trying to get this bandage in place."

The other thug spoke through a perpetual sneer. "Don't waste your time, Doc. He won't be needing it."

She continued her work as she answered, "You want him to bleed all over the place?"

"I guess not. Finish up fast."

She continued working calmly. "I don't know who you are and I don't like you frightening the hell out of my patients." Her voice had a tone of menace.

"Sorry, Doc. But we have business with your patient."

"You could have waited outside." As she spoke she put on the last strip of tape. Instead of using the scissors to cut the tape, she used a scalpel.

The two hoods laughed at the ridiculousness of her suggestion. But knowing who she was, they were polite. After all, they might need some medical treatment one day, too.

"Get down and I'll help you into your jacket," she told Bolan.

"What about my shirt?"

"It's too bloody."

With the scalpel still in her hand, she walked to the sink and picked up the bloody shirt.

"Look!" she commanded. Then she threw the shirt over the head of the closest hood.

The second goon was distracted by the toss of the shirt. Then he remembered that he should be watching the prisoner. He should have remembered sooner.

He swung back to find that he was staring a long silencer right in the eye. It was a fascinating sight; he watched it for the rest of his life.

The discreet cough of the 93-R sounded loud in the small office. The door to the waiting room was still open. There could be no doubt that the sound had carried out there.

"What the hell was that?" a male voice asked.

A sawed-off shotgun appeared around the doorway, and the voice said, "Throw out your weapon or I make mincemeat out of the doctor."

At that moment, the door to the hallway opened. Bolan saw the edge of the twin barrels sag as the butcher's attention was momentarily distracted. Bolan, his hand, his eye and the weapon were one. The opportunity and Bolan's reaction were a single event. His finger stroked the trigger lightly and two 115-grain avengers smashed into the shotgun, knocking it off target.

Both barrels blazed their anger. Bolan didn't wait to check the results. He was through the door, into the waiting room. To Bolan's right, one goon stood by the door to the hall.

Melody was halfway in the door with packages in her arm. On his left, stood a stunned hyena, holding a smoking, sawed-off shotgun. There was no sign of the receptionist.

Bolan fired across his body, clearing the gunman's sinuses for him. The goon and bits of brain formed a neat test pattern on the ceiling.

The hulk at the door moved with surprising decision. He curled an apelike arm around Melody and yanked her in front of him for a shield. His gun dug in under her jaw. The finger whitened as he increased trigger pull.

"So much as a breath of air and she gets it," he rasped. "Drop your piece."

Bolan had little choice. He could hit the giant around Melody's slight body, but there was too much pressure on the trigger. He could bet that the dying spasm would decapitate Melody. Bolan dropped the 93-R.

"You get out here, too, Doc. I figure you're involved in this," he called. Then turning his head toward the door, he said, "Come in and help, Nino. The others have bought the biscuit."

The door opened wider and a grinning shark entered, carrying a Thompson subgun. "You're going to die slow," he told Bolan. "Real slow."

17

After Bolan and Megrims left, Johnny climbed out of the bus to slide in behind the wheel. Glancing after his brother, he saw two men get out of a white Cadillac and follow Mack into the building. Johnny casually reached back into the van and pulled out the secondhand suitcase.

"Ed, will you gas up and meet me back here? I've got something urgent to do."

Twichen, suspicion etched on his face, glanced sharply at Johnny. "What's up?"

"I want to sweep C.C.'s backtrail. If he weren't so hurt, he'd order such security precautions himself."

"I'll go with you."

Johnny shrugged. "If you do that, we'll just have to take time to get gas after C.C. comes out of Volta's office. We'd be wasting time. There's a lot we have to do before we can get Patricia away from Schizzetto. Gas up and let me do my job."

"Okay," Twichen agreed reluctantly. He climbed into the driver's seat, ignoring the twenty-dollar bill Johnny was thrusting toward him. The prince of kiddy porn drove away, doing his best to make the tires squeal with the underpowered engine.

Johnny strode past the white Caddy, pretending not to notice the two mobsters watching him. As soon as he entered the building, he stood before the glass-fronted building directory as if looking for an office number.

He was just in time to see the driver of the white Caddy come through the doors. He was pimply-faced and wore a purple sports shirt. Johnny glanced around, looking for a battlefield, careful not to glance in the direction of the young hood. He decided the stairs to the basement would take him away from bystanders and witnesses.

Before Johnny had reached the bottom of the stairs, he heard shoes on the steel steps behind him. He found himself in a narrow hall with cinder-block walls, which had been painted a sickly yellow. The few doors in the hall led to storage and maintenance areas; the two Johnny tried were locked. Ahead of him was a door, the top half of which was wire-reinforced safety glass. Beyond it was underground parking for the doctors' cars. Johnny tried the handle. The door was locked.

Johnny turned. Ten feet away, the pimply-faced mobster in the purple shirt was grinning with unadulterated joy. He held a wicked-looking knife in front of him. The blade was narrow, gleaming and at least seven inches long.

Johnny held the cheap suitcase in his left hand. The Nambu was in his belt, but he didn't dare risk using a weapon. The long corridor would amplify the noise of a shot. There was little chance that Johnny could use a gun and get out of the building without being seen. Besides, his principal objective was to get to Mack and warn him. That had to be accomplished quickly, or it would be too late.

Art Rocca came in with the knife low and his arms wide. The corridor was too narrow for significant sideways maneuvering. Johnny gripped the case, with the handle resting across the back of his knuckles. He waved it in front of him like a shield, hoping the punk would be stupid enough to lunge with the knife.

The knife fighter was more experienced than that. He kept trying to slash Johnny's hand, but didn't thrust hard enough for the knife to penetrate the case. It was only a matter of seconds before Rocca would manage his objective or find another way of breaking through Johnny's inadequate defense.

Under the cover of the suitcase, Johnny drew the Japanese automatic from his belt, holding it out of sight. When the moment was right, he reached around the temporary shield and flipped the gun at his opponent. The knife never wavered, but remained stationary while the knifeman caught the gun in his left hand.

The grin of triumph turned to a shout of rage when Johnny thrust the suitcase at the stiletto with both hands, impaling it on the blade. Johnny plunged toward his opponent, who was unable to back up fast enough to yank the knife from the case.

The pressure on the knife hand was unyeilding. Johnny twisted the case. Fighting to keep his balance, the punk pulled the trigger of the Nambu. Nothing happened. Johnny had deliberately left the safety on.

Even then, Rocca might have recovered, but Johnny's trap was too alluring. Fumbling for the safety on the unfamiliar weapon, the thug broke concentration.

Johnny, who had been waiting for that small lapse, launched himself forward. The mobster's arms windmilled as he fought to recover his balance, leaving his body wide open.

Johnny raised the suitcase and executed a perfect punt. The sound as Rocca's head hit the cement floor told Johnny that one Mafia knife artist would never terrify anyone again.

The ex-Marine scooped up the automatic and tucked it back in his belt. He ripped the left shirt sleeve from the corpse and unfastened an arm sheath. He quickly fastened the sheath on his own arm, yanked the stiletto from the side of the suitcase and snugged it in the sheath. After letting his sleeve back down, he retrieved the suitcase and left the basement, whistling.

No one in the lobby looked like a mobster. The ever useful directory referred Johnny to the eighteenth floor, and an elevator carried him there quickly. Stepping off the elevator, Johnny spotted the dark-blue pinstripe from the white Cadillac.

The wearer of the suit looked like a banker who was gleefully about to dispossess some young widow of the family homestead. The reason for the glee was the Thompson subgun he was pulling from under a light coat draped over his arm.

Johnny was in an open hallway. There was no chance of pulling a gun before the Thompson splattered him along the walls. So he did the only thing he could: he moved forward as if encountering a man sporting an automatic weapon was so commonplace that it escaped his notice.

He swung the cheap suitcase in front of him as if examining the latch, again hoping to use it to cover his right hand as it drew the automatic from his belt. Johnny had been told that Fortune favored the brave; he was wondering how she felt about the foolhardy. Still, he could see no other option.

Before the mobster could tear his affectionate gaze from his Thompson, a blast shook the door behind him. He pushed the door open with great caution.

Johnny rapidly closed the gap between himself and the mobster. He heard a voice inside croak, "So much as a breath of air and she gets it. Drop the damn gun."

As Johnny lengthened his stride, he heard the same voice call out, "Come in and help, Nino. The others have bought the biscuit."

The one called Nino thrust open the door and stepped in. His grin of triumph told Johnny that Nino's concentration was focused entirely on the office and the people inside.

Johnny glided the last few steps to the door as Nino said, "You're going to die slow, real slow."

Quickly glancing up and down the hall, Johnny was shocked to find that no one down the hall had appeared to investigate the blast. As he stepped sideways through the doorway, Nino was directly in front of him. To Johnny's left, a huge gorilla held a Colt to Melody's head. Both men were watching Mack Bolan.

"You're both coming with us," Nino said.

"Take the Doc, too. She's in on this," Vito Baccliono said. His voice might have been a rusty hinge.

Johnny drew the Nambu with his left hand. That put the thumb safety on the side opposite his thumb. He had to use his right hand to flick off the safety.

Bolan understood his brother's awkward position at a glance. He straightened up and let his arms drop slowly to his sides.

"Put 'em up." Baccliono insisted.

Nino took the slack out of the Thompson's trigger. Both men's concentration centered more completely on Bolan.

Johnny slipped the safety, then held the stiletto at waist height. He gently closed the door with his foot. The click of the door was not an alarming sound. As Nino turned toward the disturbance, Johnny thrust the knife forward into Nino's kidney.

Nino had no more interest in Bolan or in the Thompson, which dropped unfired from his fingers. The Mafia killer was totally absorbed in the agony that radiated from his back, an agony so intense that nothing else mattered.

As soon as the knife slid home, Johnny paid no further attention to Nino. He brought his left arm out straight into a single-handed target stance, lining the gun sight on Baccliono's temple.

He caught the falling motion with the corner of his eye and swiveled his head in time for his eyes to record the muzzle-flash of a handgun. The bullet entered his forehead. He never had time to figure out what the muzzle-flash meant. His grip on the weapon and on Melody relaxed. He slipped down to the floor like a deflated toy.

Melody twisted while the Mafia goon collapsed. She let out a piercing scream of horror. Before anyone could react, she bit it off, sobbed once and then took a deep breath.

"Sorry," she said.

Volta appeared in the door to the inner office. She caught her breath before asking, "Where's Gail?"

"Who?" Johnny asked.

"My nurse. What happened to her?"

In answer to the name, a head of carroty hair slowly rose from under the desk. The redhead stared silently at the three bodies on the floor.

"I'll have a lot of explaining to do when the police connect me to these creeps. Dealing with the police, the medical association and the syndicate is more than I can handle." Dr. Volta's voice was stiff, formal. Bolan could see how close she was to tears.

"You can simply disappear," he told her. "When the police find this mess, they'll presume you've been taken by the Mob."

"I have a responsibility to my patients."

To everyone's surprise, the receptionist spoke up. "There aren't that many critical cases. Most of them will find other surgeons without harm. I'll bet there aren't more than six or eight patients who are critical right now. And Dr. Young will handle those."

"If you take the files, police will think it's a reason for the crime," Johnny said. "Who's going to believe the Mob then, if they claim you're one of them? You have a good chance of coming out clean."

While they spoke, Bolan put on the new shirt and jacket that Melody had bought for him. By the time he slipped the jacket over his shoulder rig, it was decided.

"Melody, you and Edgar go back to your friend's apartment. I have some business with The Picker. If we're not back by supper, get out of town. But don't show up at any bus or train stations, or at the airport."

She nodded, but said nothing.

"Where will I find The Picker at his time of day?" Bolan asked.

"Simon Fraser University. The library steps. Students in the know can always find him there at this time of year," Megrims told him.

"What can we do for you?" he asked the doctor.

She paused from her conversation with her nurse only long enough to smile and shake her head.

Bolan, Johnny and Megrims left the office. Johnny closed the door on the surgeon and nurse, who were collecting files.

On the way down in the elevator, Johnny said, "The slime with the Thompson was carrying this as a back-up gun. You'd better keep this in your purse, but don't let Twichen see it. I'm not quite ready to trust him with a gun again."

Melody knew Twichen's bullets had gone dangerously wild, one of them striking the taxi cab. It helped some that Johnny understood, but it didn't help much.

Johnny didn't notice her silence. He said to Bolan, "I took care of one more. He followed me into the building. Two cars at four mugs per car means that each car probably has a driver still sitting, waiting."

Megrims pulled herself away from her haunting thoughts and said, "We can't leave them there to move in on Volta and her nurse."

Johnny looked at her and grinned. "What do you think we should do about it?"

Melody wasn't as easily put off. "I think you two should do something about it, but if you don't, I will. Dr. Volta doesn't deserve what will happen to her for helping you."

"Easy," Bolan told her. "We wouldn't do that to the good lady, either."

"We'll have to be quick; they're using CBs," Johnny said.

"I'll take care of the one in front of the building. You and Melody handle the other one. I'll drive by so you can follow me in the other Cadillac."

"Why not just leave them?"

"They're too broad a path to Schizzetto. I don't want the police getting there before we do."

"Are you up to it?" Johnny asked.

"I have to be." Bolan turned to Melody as they stepped from the elevator. "We'll leave before you do. Go back to Shirley's with Twichen. We'll call soon."

As Johnny and Melody headed toward the parking lot, he spoke to her in a soft voice, "When we leave here, walk to the passenger side of the car and start to climb in the front seat."

She bit her lip, pulled her shoulders straight, then nodded her willingness to help.

Luigi gawked as the two walked from the building. Johnny stopped by the right front fender to search his pocket. Megrims continued to the car, opened the door and got in.

Johnny moved like a flash to the open driver's window. The captured stiletto slid in between Luigi's first and second vertebra, cutting off all communication between the brain and body.

Luigi spasmed once, then went limp over the wheel.

"Get going!" There was quiet urgency in Johnny's voice.

He opened the driver's door and pushed the small hood onto the floor on the passenger side, then slid behind the wheel. Melody closed the other door and walked toward the van. Johnny started the Cadillac, praying his brother would not take too long.

Mack Bolan walked from the front of the building with the casualness of a man who has nothing on his mind. He spotted the other white Cadillac parked across the street and strolled across the road to the driver's side of the car. The window was rolled down.

The pace was so nonchalant that the driver didn't notice Bolan until he was five feet away. A hand flew to the left armpit and the beady eyes did a quick assessment of the crowds to see whether he could risk shooting.

"If you pull that gun, you'll have to leave your friends stranded," Bolan told him.

It took two seconds for the thug to reason that Bolan's appearance meant his fellow jackals would not be returning. Two seconds stretched into eternity. Bolan forcefully seized the goon's chin and turned it until he faced straight ahead. Then the extended middle knuckle of his left fist connected with the goon's temple with all the force he could muster. The blow traveled such a short distance, no one noticed it.

Bolan opened the car door and slid the body into the passenger seat. He climbed in and anchored the lifeless form with the seat belt. Just another sleeping passenger in a comfortable car. The Executioner started the car.

Melody saw the two white Cadillacs drive from the parking lot just as she climbed into the van.

Twichen asked, "Where's Corsaro and Johnny?"

"There was some trouble. Let's get out of here."

Twichen made no effort to start the van. "What happened? Are they okay?"

"As okay as you can be with two infected bullet wounds. They've hijacked two of Schizzetto's cars and have gone to do something. They didn't say what."

Twichen pounded the steering wheel in angry frustration. "Why the hell do I miss out on the action? You get to help out, but little Eddy's left to sit in the car."

"I wish I'd been left to sit in the car. Some animal practically stuck his gun through my jaw and started to pull the trigger. Johnny shot him first. You're welcome to all the action you want. Just leave me out of it."

"Now they've gone to rescue Patricia without me. I'm not going to be treated like a child!"

Melody bit off the obvious reply. "I don't think that's where they went."

"What are they going to do? Let her rot?"

"I don't know, but I trust them."

Twichen opened the door and stepped out. "You may trust them, but I don't. Someone has to do something around here."

"Eddy, come back!"

He gave her a withering look and stalked off. She thought of going after him, but it would be foolish to make a big scene while she had a gun in her purse and was next to a building containing half a dozen bodies.

She slid into the driver's seat. She could only go back to Shirley's apartment, and be there when C.C. and Johnny arrived. She started the engine and drove away carefully, worried about the hotheaded Twichen.

18

Melody arrived back at Shirley Queen's apartment just in time to join her for the first coffee of her day. Shirley had been living at the house on Jackson Street when Melody was being introduced into the wonders and delights of being a Mob hooker. Although Shirley was a year younger than Melody, she was more experienced and had helped Melody adjust without too many beatings from The Picker.

"Where are your friends?" Shirley asked.

"Out making trouble for the Mob."

"Don't joke, Melody. You don't know how rough those creeps can play."

Melody stirred her coffee for several minutes while she thought. She felt she owed Shirley, but knew that the hooker wasn't to be trusted with the lives of her friends.

"They had eight men at the doctor's office, waiting to kill us. That's how rough they play."

"You're kidding." Shirley studied her guest's face. She said in a quieter voice, "You're not kidding. How did you get away?"

"You'll read about it in the papers. It's not important. What matters is that we're a danger to you if we stay here. The Mob's not going to be gentle if they find out you sheltered us."

Shirley said, "So I boot you out. Where do you go?"

"We have to get out of one more person's clutches. When we do that, we're all headed down to San Diego. I'm going to get a straight job there. Why don't you come and do the same?"

"No thank you. I know what happens to girls who run away. I don't want acid in the face and I don't want to be sold to the Arabs."

"C.C. and Johnny know what they're doing. We'll make it."

"What have you been smoking?"

"I'm clean, Shirley. And my head's clearer than it's ever been. I owed The Picker some bread and couldn't pay the vigorish. But he didn't make me a hooker. I did that. I had lots of ways out, but didn't have the guts to take them."

"It's called survival."

"No! It's called cowardice. Damn, Shirley! That C.C. is hurting so bad, I don't know how he stands up. But he keeps going and he looks after me and a couple of the young porn actors. He doesn't have these problems. I don't believe he ever took the easy way out of anything. You know why?"

"I can guess. Anyone who walks through eight of the Mob's goons must fight like Attila the Hun."

Melody laughed. "I can't say you're wrong, but I don't think that's the main reason. Both C.C. and Johnny do what they have to do, and they're so sure they're doing the right thing, nothing can stop them."

Shirley whistled. "You're either loco or in love. Probably both." She reached over and switched on the television. "Time for news. I always watch to find out what the johns are talking about."

The announcer was talking excitedly about live coverage from their mobile unit. On the screen, corpses were being carried from a building and loaded into a large van, which served as a multiple ambulance.

The announcer mentioned six bodies, five found in the office of an eminent surgeon who, with her receptionist, was missing. Someone had looted the offices. The announcer then interviewed the chief of police, who was just arriving on the scene.

The reporter tried to get the police chief to comment on the possible relationship between this "massacre" and the bullet-riddled bodies found in a film studio where firemen had been called earlier that morning.

The chief muttered something about underworld figures and excused himself, saying there would be a statement later.

Shirley reached over and turned off the set.

"Your friends did that?"

Melody nodded.

"And they're taking you out of here?"

Melody nodded again. "Johnny promised I could go south with him when he takes Patricia home. He'll help find me a job."

"You're stuck on him, aren't you?"

Melody smiled and shook her head. "He's nice, but..." Her voice trailed off.

"But what?"

"But wait until you see his big brother."

"Why aren't you going with him?"

Melody looked confused and shook her head. "He'll probably come along. But there's something remote about him. Some place no one can touch."

Shirley nodded. "I know what you mean. Sometimes men are like that when they've lost someone that really meant a lot to them."

"In that case, he's lost several someones, but one in particular, I think."

After another sip Shirley asked, "When do we leave?"

Just then the apartment buzzer sounded. They sat in frozen silence, unwilling to use the intercom to the lobby. Someone else must have opened the front door, because minutes later there was a knock on the apartment door.

EDGAR TWICHEN PAID OFF THE TAXI while he was still several blocks from Schizzetto's. He then walked up the road until he came to the driveway through the bush. Soon he reached the fence. It never occurred to him that it might either be electrified or attached to an alarm system. There was a flower bed on the other side. He took the revolver from under his shirt and tossed it into the flower bed, without touching the fence. He was less cautious about noise on the way back to the road, but the dampness and fog still befriended him.

When he regained the road, he cheerfully walked along the driveway until he came to the gate. When a guard emerged, he asked for Miss Dane.

"No one here by that name," the guard growled.

"She's here," Twichen contradicted. "Mr. Hanchovini sent me to coach her for her next role."

The guard said nothing, but opened a box on the inside of the gate post and picked up a handset. There was a muffled conversation.

When he came back, the guard opened the gate to admit the young porn star, slamming it shut the second he was through.

"Grab the bars and spread your legs," he said.

"What do you mean?"

"I got orders, buddy. You don't go nowhere until I know you're clean."

Twichen did as he was told. When the guard was through with him, Twichen walked up the driveway until the fog enveloped him. Then he took to the grass and ran to the flower bed. After his gun was tucked under his shirt once more, Twichen ran back until he found the driveway again. Then he resumed walking.

He was met at the front door by a six-foor-four specimen in a dark-blue suit.

"I'm here to see Miss Dane," Twichen said.

"Mr. Schizzetto wants to talk to you," the big man told him.

Twichen cocked his head to one side. "Are you the butler? What do I call you?"

The houseman looked at the young punk and smirked. "I'm the security chief. You call me 'sir.'"

Twichen silently followed Louis into a living room.

Little Squirt didn't waste time on preliminaries. "Who told you Dane was here, kid?"

Kid? Twichen hated the Mafia Don. "Mr. Hanchovini sent me. He said we had to get back to work tomorrow and I'd better make sure she was letter perfect."

Schizzetto tapped his teeth with a ball point pen while he eyed the young actor. It was possible that Hanchovini had sent him. Frankie Hanky had enough sense to ask permission.

More to the point, Hanky was buzzard meat and Little Squirt had on his hands another young punk who knew where to find Frankie's boss.

Twichen shifted uncomfortably while the Don sat and eyed him. The young porn star thought about elaborating his story, but decided to remain silent.

Before Twichen showed up, Little Squirt had decided to get out of porn for a year or so. The police were all over Lion's Gate Productions and would know by now what the chief product was. The problem was to make sure all his connections with the studio were buried. That meant burying the Dane broad and this junior stud. But first the turkey doctor would have to take them apart. After these two had screamed their lungs out for a few days, Schizzetto would know the names of everyone who knew of his connection to Lion's Gate Productions. Then they could all be silenced.

"Put them both in the guest room," he told Louis. "See that someone attends them." "Attends them" was household parlance for listening in on the hidden microphones in "the guest room." It was called that because it was set up to record on tape and videotape everything that happened in the room. The "guest room" and a few floozies had certainly paid for themselves in terms of political clout.

Louis nodded and hustled Twichen out of the room. The young hero didn't resist; he was being taken to where he could protect Patricia.

There was one small hitch in Twichen's plans. Dane still believed she was on her way to stardom. She had no intention of being rescued. In vain, Twichen pleaded with her, showed her his gun, told her that C.C. and Johnny would soon get then out.

Forty minutes later, Dane pounded on the door demanding to be taken to Schizzetto, but the Don wasn't interested. He'd already heard the tapes.

He looked up at Louis and said, "You heard. Tell the boys a couple of horses' asses will be along soon to spring our guests. I want those two saved for our turkey doctor as well. Are The Picker's boys ready to come up the mountain and seal the place off?"

Louis nodded.

Little Squirt grinned. "Should be an entertaining evening."

19

In an underground parking lot, Bolan and Johnny transferred the two corpses to the trunk of Bolan's Caddy. From there they drove straight to Simon Fraser and stopped in the "no parking" zone in front of the library.

Pico Pellico was sitting on the library steps, pretending to read a book. With his ponytail, sweatshirt and jeans, he could almost pass as a student. He looked up when the two cars stopped, his face puzzled.

Waving for Johnny to stay put, Bolan turned off the ignition and removed the keys. He idly tossed them in the air and caught them as he approached The Picker.

"C.C., it's good to see you up and about. How's the shoulder?"

Bolan sat on the steps beside The Picker before replying, "Better. It's coming down, Pico. I want to know where you stand."

"What's that supposed to mean? We're friends, ain't we?"

"I hope so. Those were Little Squirt's cars, weren't they?"

"Were?"

Bolan ignored the question. "He didn't supply them to your men, by any chance?"

"What's this about, C.C.? My men don't drive anything that flashy."

"I thought so. I had to ask."

"It's time you told me what this is all about."

Bolan sat silently. The Picker began to fidget. The Executioner finally said, "You're right. You should know what's coming down. There was a crew of four in each of those cars. They were sent to punch my ticket."

"Eight of 'em! Where are they?"

"Slabbed."

The Picker swallowed, but didn't say anything.

"If he sent those, he'd also take precautions, in case his plan got screwed up. Is he taking precautions, Pico?

The Picker stared at his book, as if he'd find the answer there. Bolan could almost read his mind. Pellico would be figuring some way to stay neutral and then convince the winner he was on his side all along.

"He was your Don, Pico, but you don't owe loyalty to the dead."

The Picker started. "He's dead?" It was both an exclamation and a question.

"He knew why I was here. Those eight soldiers just pleaded guilty for him. The sentence was passed. He's still breathing, but he's dead."

"Yeah, he's taking precautions. Not only has he his own crew to bottle his place, he's got twenty of my boys farther down the mountain to act as backup."

"I'll give you a reason to withdraw them. When you get the reason, do it."

"What sort of a reason?"

"You'll know it when you see it. What about money, Pico?"

"It takes a lot of cash to rebuild an organization. The West Coast don't operate on peanuts. The man who rebuilds and takes over will have to pay the troops, keep the grease on the politicians, send his share of council's expenses and build the business. Have you got enough capital to step in?"

The Picker felt excitement and despair at the same time. C.C. was offering him a chance to pick up the West Coast operation, but he hadn't thought about the money before.

After the mobster had stewed for several seconds, Bolan asked, "Who's the local banker?"

"Wally Wonta. He collects for the East. He advances money to Little Squirt for big projects. He also finances the layoff betting for the bookies. No one but the Don can borrow money through him."

"I'll speak to him. Sometimes future Dons have been known to get loans. No guarantees, but I figure it will clear with New York, if I go out on the limb. Will he have enough on hand?"

The Picker shrugged. He was too excited to speak.

Bolan was still tossing the car keys in his left hand. He suddenly flipped them in front of Pellico, who caught them.

"I guess the cars are as good as yours," Bolan said. "May I borrow one? I'll go talk to Wonta."

Pellico nodded.

Bolan left without saying more and climbed into the Caddy beside Johnny.

"Downtown. How much in your wallet?"

"About two hundred Canadian."

"That should do for a deposit. You need a suit and all the trimmings. Let me have the cash."

"What's wrong with jeans? You're wearing them."

"Perfect for a raid. Terrible for fading into the woodwork."

Johnny shrugged and forked over the cash. Bolan searched until he found a men's wear store where none of the lines included anything in the lower price range.

"That store. Don't park too close. If they see a Caddy, they'll sell you any old junk."

"We're going in there looking like this?" Johnny asked.

"What's wrong with jeans?" Bolan fed back to him.

They stepped into the store. A salesman, looking as if he were dressed to run a mortuary, hurried forward.

"My young friend's luggage was stolen," Bolan explained. "I'm giving a dinner tonight, not formal. There's $200 in it for you if you can completely outfit him by six."

"Then a business suit should be about right. I think we have a few on the rack—"

"On the rack!" Bolan interrupted.

"Please," begged the clerk, "you must understand. There simply isn't time to have a suit ready in four hours. However, these are really fine imported materials and our tailors are good. No one will know the suit hasn't been through three fittings."

Bolan looked quizzically at Johnny, who shrugged. He turned his attention back to the salesman.

"Okay," Bolan said.

Johnny chose a suit he'd be happy to wear in court. "Not a bad fit," he commented.

The clerk gave him a horrified look and practically ran to the back of the store. In a moment, he re-emerged with two ancient tailors who swarmed over Johnny.

Bolan slipped the $200 to the clerk. "Choose the accessories. I mean everything. Get him shoes, too."

The money vanished. "Everything will be waiting by six, sir," the clerk assured him.

"Where to now?" Johnny asked as they left the store.

"West Coast Finance."

They drove in tense silence. Bolan had the battered suitcase open on his lap and was doing a pre-battle check of the weapons.

Johnny pulled the car to the curb on a shoddy street by the waterfront near their destination. As they got out, Johnny checked to make sure the Japanese automatic in his belt didn't show. He took the suitcase.

West Coast Finance occupied the second floor of an older brick building. Bolan and Johnny walked through the office door.

"Tell Mr. Wonta that Corsaro Cancellari is here from New York to see him."

The receptionist looked at Bolan in his plaid shirt and jeans and said, "Mr. Wonta's busy. Can I help you?"

"Yes," he said. "You can tell Mr. Wonta that if he leaves me standing here for over two minutes, I'm going in there to kick his balls off. You tell him that."

The receptionist knew how to deal with threats. She met them often, usually from people Wonta referred to a Mr. Pellico for financing. She reached for the buzzer under the counter.

A large, strong hand seized her wrist before she reached the alarm. Blue eyes, looking into hers, glistened with cold power.

"We're being set up," Bolan told Johnny. "Watch the door."

Johnny followed his instructions by pulling the Nambu and opening the door a crack so he could watch the hall. At the sight of the gun, the office staff of four let out a collective gasp.

"Everyone over by the wall," Bolan commanded, gesturing with a gun. "If anyone comes down the hall, you're all dead."

They moved slowly, cautiously, putting their hands in the air without being told. Bolan covered them with one of the captured Mafia Colt automatics while he crossed the office. He didn't try the door handle to the inner office. He simply booted the door open, smashing the catch.

"Out here, Wonta," he commanded the startled man at the desk. "We're taking you back to New York."

Looking puzzled and not a little worried, the pudgy manager slowly left the office.

"You're dead," Wonta told Bolan.

"That may be what you planned," Bolan answered, "but you're leaving with us now. When your ambush boys show up, you either talk us through or you're the first to go. You're probably dead anyway when New York finds out you engineered this heist."

Wonta was completely mystified. He wasn't engineering a heist; these two strangers were waving guns about. Yet they hadn't mentioned taking any money.

"What do you want?" Wonta asked.

"For starters, to get out of here with our hides and Sammy Sling's money intact. After that, it's up to Sammy to have you rubbed out."

Wonta knew Sammy Sling. He was head of the dope distribution out of New York—not a pleasant character to cross. But Wonta, the Mafia banker for the Canadian West Coast, didn't have any of Sammy's money.

"I don't know what you're talking about. There's none of Sammy's money here."

"Oh yeah! What do you call that?" Bolan pointed to the old suitcase in Johnny's hand.

The strange turn of events was affecting the staff. They looked at each other, puzzled. Who would have thought that their diminutive boss would start arguing with a couple of men with guns?

"I'm confused," Wally admitted. "Are you from Sammy?"

"You know damn well we are."

"How would I know that?"

"Because Sammy phoned Little Squirt and arranged to have his million held cool until the shipment comes in. We walk in with the cash, and suddenly no one knows us. You may get the money, Wonta, but Sammy isn't going to be overjoyed."

"I wasn't told about any money for safekeeping."

"Sure you weren't." Bolan spoke up to Johnny. "His goons coming down the hall yet?"

"No sign of anyone."

"What's wrong, Wonta? Don't tell me you were stupid enough to depend on your secretary over there to flash the alarm. She was too obvious."

"I tell you, no one told me to expect you. If all you want is a safe place for the cash, no problem."

"Something stinks. Where's your hard boys, Wonta?"

"There are no hard boys. There's been a misunderstanding. Let me phone Mr. Schizzetto and straighten it out."

"You touch that telephone and you're dead."

Wonta was nearly crying from a combination of fear and frustration. "I tell you there was a foul-up. No one's trying to hijack Sammy's money."

Bolan hesitated.

"Still no one coming," Johnny told him.

"There's no one coming," Wonta insisted.

"You'll give us a receipt we can send to Sammy for insurance?"

"You know we don't make receipts for this type of thing."

"Move, Wonta. You go down the stairs first. When the bullets fly, I want you in the middle."

"Shit! I tell you there'll be no bullets flying. Okay. Okay! I'll sign a receipt, but I got to see it mailed. I don't want you trigger-happy types carrying it around. If Vancouver police found it, they'd close this front down.''

"Okay. Store this with the emergency bag.''

"It'll be okay in the regular safe.''

"Let's go Wonta. I knew I couldn't trust you. We're going for a short trip together.''

The pudgy gang banker was perspiring.

"All right. You've caused enough trouble. If I give you a receipt and I put this in my private safe, will you be satisfied?''

Bolan thought about that for a long time. He rendered his decision just in time to save the small hood from a heart attack.

"Okay.''

Wonta let out a long breath. "My office.''

Before Bolan disappeared into the inner office, he told Johnny, "Get the staff to work.'' Then he took the suitcase of weapons, stepped inside the inner office and shut the door.

Wonto immediately slid back a small panel in the wall. "I should count it before I give you a receipt,'' he said.

"Open the safe so you can shove it in if someone comes,'' Bolan said. He opened the suitcase on Wonta's desk. It was above the kneeling man, and he couldn't see the contents.

Wonta hid the dial of the safe with his body, as he spun the combination and pulled the door open. While he was busy with the safe, Bolan dropped the Colt 1911 into the case and drew the silenced Beretta.

When the safe was open, he told Wonta, "Now put the briefcase on the desk.''

Wonta's hand hovered over a briefcase in the safe and then flashed out holding a hideaway .38 revolver. The Beretta whispered once, punching a hole through his spinal column at the neck. He was knocked forward, partly into the safe.

Bolan holstered the 93-R and stepped over to the safe. A cursory examination convinced him that there were enough papers in the safe to let the police know who Wonta really worked for. He closed and latched the old suitcase, then checked the briefcase on the desk. It was filled with Canadian bills, used and with no sequential serial numbers. Bolan estimated that it contained at least a quarter million dollars.

With the suitcase in one hand and the briefcase in the other, he left the office.

Johnny had put the staff to work. All the ledgers, loan records and other paperwork were stacked in the middle of the floor.

"You can go now," Bolan told them. "The first one out has to turn on the fire alarm."

The receptionist didn't get it. "What fire?"

Bolan gestured to Johnny who had just put a match to the pile of papers. The office workers decided it really was time to leave.

Johnny and Bolan followed them down at a leisurely pace, walked to the Caddy and drove away.

"What now?" Johnny asked.

"Now let's go buy a car."

20

Cash payment was of great interest to the Mercedes dealer. When he found that the cash would cover the list price of the car, no matter the amount shown on the contract, he was delighted.

He had no trouble assuring his customer that the elegant sedan would be waiting at five-thirty that afternoon, licensed, insured and fueled. The dealer photostated Johnny's California driver's license for the necessary information.

Back in the Caddy, Johnny asked, "I can see that driving back with swank clothes, in an expensive car is good cover, but what's going to happen to my Volkswagen?"

"I'll take that."

"What's the point of buying a Mercedes, if you're going to follow us over the border in my van?"

"I'll head east. We want to give the Mafia something to pursue."

"Oh, no you won't!"

"Pull up at that pay phone."

Johnny did as he was told, but he was worried. Mack's energy wouldn't last forever. He still had a lot of healing and recovering to do. But Johnny knew better than to argue. Besides, who knew how well things would go at Schizzetto's? There was a good chance both of them would be buried in Vancouver. The thought made Johnny shudder. Being killed was one thing, but being buried here!

Bolan stepped back into the Caddy. "Melody and Shirley will go shopping and be suitably dressed to accompany you," he told Johnny.

"And Shirley?"

"Melody talked her into giving up her career in public service."

"Melody must know how to talk to people," Johnny commented in a dry voice.

"One other piece of news," Bolan said, "Eddy Twichen isn't there. He decided to rescue his princess on his own."

"Shit!"

"It's going to be flying thick. Let's go."

"Where to next?"

"We have an appointment with Little Squirt."

"I thought we were going to wait until dawn," Johnny commented as he turned the Cadillac toward West Vancouver.

"We were. We can no longer afford the luxury."

"Mack?"

"Yeah?"

"Are you up to this?"

"I have to be, don't I?"

The two warriors circled past Shirley's apartment. They abandoned the Caddy and took the Volkswagen from the garage.

"They're going to recognize this," Johnny said as they drove for North Vancouver.

Bolan shrugged. He was checking out the weapons.

They found themselves slowed down by the early rush-hour traffic over Lion's Gate Bridge.

"If we were half an hour later, it would take another hour to get over the bridge," Johnny explained.

Bolan was scanning the route. "Too many large cars at that motel," he remarked.

"You think that's where Pico's troops are staying? I thought he agreed to use the raid as an excuse to pull them back."

"He didn't agree. He just didn't say 'no.' It doesn't matter, he wouldn't have kept his word anyway. I just thought I'd give him the chance. Stop at the next pay phone."

Bolan's phone call lasted forty seconds.

"You give The Picker hell?" Johnny asked.

"Uh-huh. I also told the police where they'd find a couple of bodies. I suggested it was part of a gang war."

Johnny chuckled until he had to break it off to say, "There's the first house."

"Pull up beside the crew wagon. We don't want to block it in."

Johnny pulled the Volkswagen into the driveway beside a big Olds station wagon. It was one of the two locations where Schizzetto housed his palace guard. As the two warriors climbed from the bus, a thug in guard's uniform opened the side door.

"Waddya want?" the hood demanded.

"Peace, equality, justice for all," Johnny told him.

"You some kind of a nut?"

Bolan answered with a single 9 mm parabellum that mangled the heart on its way through the thug's body.

Johnny grabbed the dead man before he could fall. He held the corpse until Bolan could grab it by the other side. They dragged it around to the far side of the station wagon and put it in the back seat, sitting as if alive. Johnny pulled the revolver from the corpse's holster and tossed it in the bus.

When they entered the house, a voice called from the front room. "Who were they, Joe?"

Bolan appeared in the doorway of the living room where three thugs watched a baseball game on television.

"Death," Bolan told them.

Bolan's submachine gun said the same thing in a universal language. Three short utterances delivered heart-stopping messages.

Johnny turned toward the back of the house. When the MP-44 delivered its verdict in the living room, two sleepy goons appeared from bedrooms in the back. Both seemed to have been getting ready for a late-afternoon nap. Johnny soothed them back to sleep with the Japanese automatic.

A quick search of the house revealed no more occupants, although there were bunk rooms downstairs for another dozen. The rest were either on duty or among those who had gone into town in the white Cadillacs.

Johnny and Bolan took two of the corpses that were in uniform and sat them in the back seat of the station wagon to keep their brother-in-gore company. Rope from a basement clothesline held them in place. Bolan drove the crew wagon and Johnny followed in the van.

Johnny parked the Volks in the street while Bolan wheeled into the driveway of the second house that bivouacked Little Squirt's personal troops. Bolan waited until Johnny leaned on the front doorbell before putting three quiet shots into the lock. The tumbler shattered and a powerful kick smashed the door inward.

One of the hoods was pouring coffee in the kitchen. A silent parabellum entered his temple. The hood fell backward. The glass coffeepot fell on him, spilled its contents and rolled to the floor, unbroken.

The Executioner moved silently through the kitchen toward the front hall. A thug came hurrying from the back of the house to see what the commotion was. His path took him past the door to the kitchen. A hand swung from the kitchen doorway, axing the creep in the larynx. The man collapsed.

Three hoods appeared in the doorway. "What the hell?" one exclaimed.

Bolan's Beretta murmured its reply. The hood at the back of the group sprayed brains on the questioner. He spun around, reaching for his revolver.

Bolan tracked the sights to the next hood and sent the last bullets in the clip to play hopscotch on the man's spine. The guy coughed once and pushed himself back. His legs quit and he flopped backward onto the floor. Then his heart stopped and he was still.

The goon who'd acquired the extra brains was bringing up his revolver to bear. Johnny's knife discussed the point with the mobster's heart.

Johnny added two more corpses to the crew wagon, tying them into the right side of the front seat. Bolan searched the house, finding two rifles for Johnny to add to his collection of weapons in the Volkswagen.

Johnny, by prior agreement, took off for the mountain behind Schizzetto's, and Bolan moved the Oldsmobile into the garage where it couldn't be seen. Then he prowled the house for any information he could find on Mafia operations. There was nothing worth having.

Then Bolan poked through closets until he found a clean uniform jacket to fit. He didn't bother trying the pants. Judging from the specimens he'd seen, the guards were bigger than Bolan around the middle. Or else they were too short.

He glanced at his watch; twenty minutes had passed. It was time to visit Schizzetto.

Bolan climbed into the crew wagon full of stiffs and drove at a sedate pace toward the Mafia Don's estate.

Making sure Schizzetto hadn't posted sentries beyond the perimeter took longer than Johnny had counted on. The mountains behind the estate was clear of guards. Little Squirt was still depending on the electrified fence and the large clear area around the house to hold the defensive position.

Johnny unloaded his cache of weapons from the van and took out a ball of butcher's twine. He darted from bush to bush, tying weapons to trees and leading strings back from the trigger to a shallow depression behind a clump of cedars. It was tricky work to do in a hurry without revealing his position to the sentries, but he managed. He guided all the strings to where he could reach them without being seen from the house.

"STAY AWAY FROM ME!" Patricia Dane yelled. "You're nothing but loathsome scum."

Edgar Twichen shrugged. He hadn't dared to go within arms' length of her since he'd been thrust into the room. He was content to be here where he could protect her. It would be evening soon. C.C. and Johnny would come to get Patricia, but it would be Edgar Twichen who was inside with a weapon to keep her alive. It would be sweet to see Patricia eat her words when she realized he'd saved her life.

Twichen's reverie was broken by the sound of shooting from the back of the house. He was surprised that the attack was coming while it was still light; surprised but eager to be part of it.

He dragged an easy chair to a position opposite the locked door and squatted behind it, gun drawn.

"What are you doing?" Dane demanded. "Have you gone out of your skull?"

"Shut up and stay low," he told her.

She gave him a surprised look and sat on the bed.

JOHNNY OPENED PROCEEDINGS by putting a slug into one of the guards as he came around the edge of the house. The sights on the unfamiliar Savage 170 were a bit off. The 170-grain bullet punched the hood in the thigh, sending him spinning.

The sound brought another guard on the run. Adjusting for the sight, Johnny aimed above the left shoulder and scored a perfect center-chest shot.

The next two peered around the edges of the house more cautiously. Johnny amused himself by plucking strings at random. Revolvers spat lead into the yard from all over the hillside. The two latest arrivals retreated, leaving their wounded comrade lying on his back, screaming for help.

Soon a couple of windows inside the house slid up. Johnny pulled a few more strings and brought volleys of return fire. The shots came very close to the revolvers. Johnny was glad he wasn't holding them.

Mack Bolan waited until the shooting had reached a fair intensity. Then he tromped the accelerator to the floor and peeled rubber up the winding drive to Schizzetto's front gate.

The nervous guard recognized the crew wagon immediately. He squinted until he saw the six uniform jackets. With great relief, he threw open the gates to the reinforcements.

As the big wagon sped through the gates, Bolan reached across his body with the Beretta and squeezed off a three-shot burst. The second one caught the guard in the throat. He danced around the driveway in a macabre ballet of surprise and terror as his aorta spurted a stream of life two feet out from his neck.

Bolan leathered the Beretta and picked up the Swiss subgun. The 9 mm parabellums had come from this house. It was time to return them. He steered the big wagon off the driveway and over the lawn so he could circle the house, keeping it on his left.

The defenders at the side of the house looked up to see the crew wagon, full of uniforms, racing across the lawn. They cheered until controlled bursts of 9 mm tumblers knocked the cheers down their throat.

Bolan spun the wheel and the back tires spewed chunks of lawn out behind the vehicle. He raced around the back of the house and started back the other side. The surprised Mafia soldiers sprang for the wall to get out of the way of the speeding Olds.

Bolan pulled the wheel over and went roaring along the side of the brick house, scraping paint off two fenders as he went. It was a bumpy ride as the car bounced over body after body. The shouts and screams of the hoods almost succeeded in drowning out the scraping noise of fenders on brick.

As soon as he reached the front of the house again, Bolan slammed on the brakes and climbed out. He turned away from the car, deliberately leaving it in drive. The wagon moved slowly toward the front gate, drawing fire from the other side of the house and from the front.

The Executioner used a few bursts of the subgun to finish off the grisly work begun by the station wagon. Then he ran across the front of the house to the door.

Bolan's MP-44 had been tracking the windows as he ran. It finished off a hood at one of the dining-room windows. Bolan expended the last of the clip on the front door around the latch. He jammed in a fresh clip before kicking the door open.

As soon as Bolan had scattered the outside defenders, Johnny threw the MP-44 over his shoulder and ran to the wall. Flipping his jacket over a stone pillar, he scaled up one side and dropped down the other, taking his jacket with him.

An Ingram started chattering from one of the back upstairs windows. Johnny fired a short burst through the glass. The thug stood up, cursing, with a splinter of glass in his eye. Johnny paused just long enough to ease the thug's suffering and then continued to the kitchen door.

Big Tony was waiting for him, his huge hands cradling a sawed-off shotgun. He seemed fully recovered from the time Johnny had knocked him unconscious.

"I thought you'd be back, punk. I owe you one," Tony told him.

RUDOLFO SCHIZZETTO DIDN'T LIKE the way things were going. He'd increased his guard recently, but what good did it do? He tried telephoning his backup forces, but they didn't answer. Little Squirt felt the hand of Death clamping at his gut.

He put in another call to the second wave backup The Picker had supplied. To Schizzetto's relief, they answered and would leave immediately. Now, his only problem was to stay alive the five minutes it would take them to get to him through rush-hour traffic.

Why couldn't his enemy wait until night, like sensible soldiers? At night, any backup would be here in less than three minutes. The Don turned to Big Louis, the only one in the room with him. Louis had a Mac 10 in each fist.

"Let's get to the young punks. That crazy kid said this C.C. and his brother were coming to free them. If that's true, we've got some prime hostages. Let's keep them with us until The Picker's soldiers get here."

Louis nodded and led the way upstairs. About a dozen hardmen still manned the windows, but they showed no inclination to leave the house and hunt down the enemy force.

Louis unlocked the door of the guest room and flung it open. The punk kid was behind a chair, aiming a revolver at him.

"Drop the guns or I shoot," Twichen yelled. Louis, grinning, leveled one of the Ingrams.

"Watch out. It's a real gun," Dane shouted at the two mobsters.

She was frantic. If that fool Twichen killed Mr. Schizzetto, who'd put her in the movies? She ran forward, determined to protect the Mafia Don with her own body. That would stop Twichen.

Louis squeezed the trigger. Twichen shot simultaneously. Twichen's bullet hit the wall over the door, raining plaster on Schizzetto's head. Louis's clip caught Dane's running figure and tossed it back over the chair. Many of the bullets passed right through her body and lodged in the upholstered chair.

Dane's head was thrown back over the chair. Blood flowed from her mouth. Her rapidly dimming eyes were within inches of Twichen's.

"Oh, no!" he moaned. He dropped his revolver.

Louis grinned and raised the other Ingram.

BOLAN FOUND HIMSELF in the front hall, wishing he had grenades to toss through the doorways of the rooms on either side. But he had just the MP-44, his Beretta and a rapidly diminishing supply of parabellums. He ran past the two doors. There was the sound of pounding feet to his right. So he put a controlled burst through the doorway on the way past.

His burst caught two goons who had been trying to get through the door to catch Bolan. They fell back, neither interested in leaving the room.

Bolan reached the stairs to the second floor and looked back. One hood poked his head through another doorway. A short burst aerated the head.

Bolan made his way slowly upstairs, conserving his energy. Behind him, in two rooms, hoods argued about who was to have the privilege of being the next to stick his head out into the hall.

JOHNNY DIDN'T HAVE TIME to stand around while the chef settled old scores. Without breaking pace, the ex-Marine swung his subgun into the underside of the sawed-off shotgun. The first blast riddled the ceiling.

By the time Tony pulled the second trigger, Johnny had forced the gun farther back. The blast went in under Tony's chin, and it was his brains and bits of skull that went into the ceiling.

Johnny changed clips on the subgun and shouldered it. He picked up the shotgun and recharged it from a box of shells on the kitchen counter. He threw another batch of shells into his jacket pocket and eased to the door.

He paused and threw a kitchen stool through the door. A blast from the west of the house sent wood splinters flying down the hall. Johnny put the shotgun around the corner and pulled both triggers, wounding two gunmen.

Johnny reloaded and hit the floor. He then rolled into the hall, ready to blast again. It wasn't necessary. The two wounded hoods had spun 180 degrees, their agonized fingers tightening on the triggers of their subguns. Their fellow defenders shot them down.

Johnny sent two blasts into the room and reloaded once more. No one shot back. He raced to the front of the house in time to let go two charges at the hoods who had just worked up enough nerve to leave the front rooms.

Johnny dropped the empty shotgun and scooped the M-16 of one of the dead hoods. It was good to have a familiar weapon in his hands. He searched the corpses until he found a spare clip, then started upstairs.

BOLAN SAW SCHIZZETTO and his main man in the doorway to one of the rooms. He steadied himself and took a deep breath. He had to fight for control. The fight had left him weak and dizzy. While Bolan fought to steady his swaying frame, Louis emptied a clip into the room. There might have been a single shot in response. Bolan wasn't sure.

Bolan leaned against the wall, holding the Swiss submachine gun tight against his side. He took a deep breath, then as he slowly started letting it out, he triggered short bursts into the backs of both killers. The magazine and Bolan's reservoir of strength emptied at the same time. He slid down the wall, his legs too weak to hold him.

21

The house was suddenly quiet. Distant sirens told Johnny he had less than five minutes to get Mack out.

He took one quick look at Dane and wrote her off. Then he looked at Twichen. The young porn actor's face had been sprayed with blood and was now streaked with tears. He was staring at Dane's gruesome remains.

"It was my fault," he choked. "If I hadn't tried to play hero..."

"Shut up or you'll be responsible for another death. Give me a hand." Johnny's voice was cold and uncompromising.

Twichen continued to snivel.

"We've got to get out. I need your help."

Johnny dragged Bolan to his feet, supporting him by his good left shoulder. This left Johnny's right hand free to hold the MP-44.

Twichen moved forward like an automaton to support Bolan's other side.

Bolan hung between them for a moment, forcing them to take all his weight. Then slowly he willed strength into his trembling legs. They took most of the load, but were too unsteady for him to walk unaided. He still gripped the Swiss MP-44 tightly.

Johnny tugged the last full magazine from Bolan's belt and slammed it home for him. Then they tackled the stairs.

They were only a few steps on their way when two goons came around the landing from the third floor. Johnny caught the movement from the corner of his eye. Lifting the SMG, he triggered two short bursts that caught the surprised mobsters in the chest. They each turned ninety degrees, collapsing into each other. Then they sank slowly to the floor.

Downstairs, Johnny started toward the front of the house. Through the open door, he saw the first of The Picker's backup troops arrive at the gate.

"Out the back, on the double," Johnny commanded.

The iron in Johnny's voice brought an immediate response from both companions. Bolan, who was only partially conscious, started putting force into the thrust of his legs. Twichen brought his whole attention to bear on the problem of keeping Bolan upright and headed in the desired direction.

The three negotiated the back door and practically sprinted across the lawn.

One revolver barked; a bullet plucked at Johnny's sleeve. He raised the subgun behind him and blasted at the mobster. The head disappeared from the window. Whether the man was dead or simply cringing no longer mattered.

They pulled up short at the back fence.

"Watch out," Johnny warned. "It's electrified."

"Hell! I stuck my arm through it earlier today. I don't know how I didn't touch the bars."

The fence seemed much higher now that they had the problem of getting Bolan over it. While Twichen supported Bolan, Johnny climbed to the top of a stone post. He shouldered his weapon and reached for Bolan's hands.

Bolan tried twice, but was too weak to be much assistance. Then Twichen bent down and wrapped his arms around The Executioner's legs and slowly straightened, raising Bolan four feet.

The first of Pellico's troops appeared around the corner of the house, saw the three at the wall and opened fire. Twichen seemed oblivious to the bullets twanging off iron bars. Johnny assessed the range as being too far and returned his attention to Bolan.

"Hold on," Twichen grunted.

He left Johnny supporting Bolan only by the arms. The pain in Bolan's shoulder snapped his eyes wide open. Twichen bent his knees and placed Bolan's feet on his shoulders, then started to straighten again.

The four mobsters realized they were too far away to shoot accurately with automatic handguns and began to race forward, yelling for more troops to join them.

The pain recharged Bolan sufficiently and somehow brought strength to his legs. Twichen straightened, gaining the top of the pillar. Bolan, realizing too much time would be wasted trying to get him down gently, wrenched loose from Johnny and jumped. At the last moment he tucked and rolled, but the force of impact reopened the shoulder wound.

Twichen scrambled easily over the post. He jumped and grabbed Bolan, continuing to help him retreat. Johnny shouted directions while he picked up Bolan's fallen MP-44.

Johnny threw down the empty magazines, then stood waiting for the four thugs who were leading the pack to the fence. One of them was toting an Ingram; the others had only handguns. Johnny stayed behind the pillar until they were within ten feet of the fence. Then he stepped around and blasted three of them with a quick figure eight. They folded in the middle like three old suitcases.

Johnny caught up with Bolan and Twichen in time to help them the last few steps to the van. He had it set so he could release the brake and coast down the bumpy trail. Before he reached the road, he stopped the VW, started the motor and waited.

The sounds of sirens were very close. Most of Pellico's men would be bottled inside the electric fence and their weapons collected. Pellico would be busy explaining the bodies in his car.

Johnny waited until he heard more shooting. It was inevitable that a hardforce with guns out would refuse to be taken peaceably by the police. He pulled the bus onto the road, heading for West Vancouver. Several cruisers passed them, rushing to help fellow officers on the Schizzetto estate. The tactical squad passed in two hug vans.

The women were waiting at Shirley's apartment. To Johnny's surprise, so was Dr. Volta and her nurse, Gail O'Toole.

"We were terrified when she showed up at the door," Melody said. "We almost didn't open it to see who it was."

Johnny's face lost a great deal of its tension. He and Twichen supported an unconscious Bolan between them. Volta and O'Toole took charge, immediately starting to work on their patient.

"What happens now?" Melody asked.

Johnny explained Bolan's plan, then added, "I'm not sure what we're going to do now that my brother can't travel."

Volta's authoritative voice spoke from the couch where she was rebandaging Bolan's shoulder. "What would he tell you to do?"

"Carry on with the plan. But..."

"So do it. He'll be all right. He simply used more energy than he had to spare. The infection's gone. Get that car and suit before it's too late, then just get."

The two ex-prostitutes were dressed in very plain suits that made them look like junior executives. They each carried briefcases to enhance the image. They expertly guided Johnny and Twichen out of the apartment, leaving Bolan in Dr. Volta's experienced hands.

BOLAN OPENED HIS EYES to behold a massive but delightful superstructure, barely restrained by a blue shirt. He was lying on his back in a vehicle. He frowned, trying to piece together a jumbled nightmare.

"He's awake," Gail O'Toole announced.

Bolan then placed the redhead: Dr. Volta's nurse. Then the vehicle fell into place: Johnny's van.

"Who's driving?" he asked.

"Dr. Volta," O'Toole told him.

"Where are we?"

"Headed east, according to your plan."

"The others?"

"Across the border safely, looking like a million dollars." She laughed softly. "They couldn't find the right clothes for that blond young man, but he looks great in a chauffeur's uniform."

Bolan smiled. Twichen had pulled himself together well enough to play chauffeur; he'd make it. It was a safe bet that Melody would find a career in counselling; she'd persuaded Shirley into joining the group.

Suddenly, Bolan's smile faded. "It's dangerous being with me," he said.

O'Toole leaned forward and smiled. "Eleonora and I have decided to risk it. We think we'll be okay if we stick close to you. And we plan to be *really* close."

Bolan drifted back to sleep. There was a hint of a smile on his face.

MORE ADVENTURE NEXT MONTH WITH

MACK BOLAN

#87 Hellfire Crusade

Blueprint to Armageddon

The militant brother of an Arab ruler has kidnapped a brilliant young American. And Mack Bolan knows that in the wrong hands the teenager's knowledge of nuclear devices could change the course of history.

The Executioner faces awesome odds as he blitzes a forbidding desert fortress in the tiny oil sheikhdom. His mission: to rescue the hostage and stop the rebel's plans to launch a holy revolution.

DON PENDLETON's EXECUTIONER
MACK BOLAN

Sergeant Mercy in Nam . . . The Executioner in the Mafia Wars . . . Colonel John Phoenix in the Terrorist Wars . . . Now Mack Bolan fights his loneliest war! You've never read writing like this before. By fire and maneuver, Bolan will rack up hell in a world shock-tilted by terror. He wages unsanctioned war—everywhere!

Available wherever paperbacks are sold.

GOLD EAGLE

AVAILABLE NOW

#22 The World War III Game

PROJECT HOT SHOT

Everybody has something to hide when a top-secret U.S. lab inside a hollowed-out mountain has its main computer tapped by teenage hackers who have terrorist guns held to their heads.

The lab is involved in "illegal" germ-warfare research, and the Puerto Rican terrorists' plan is simple—control the lab and bring the U.S. government to its knees.

Able Team's mission: evict and destroy!

Mack Bolan's

PHOENIX FORCE

by Gar Wilson

Schooled in guerrilla warfare, equipped with all the latest lethal hardware, Phoenix Force battles the powers of darkness in an endless crusade for freedom, justice and the rights of the individual. Follow the adventures of one of the legends of the genre. Phoenix Force is the free world's foreign legion!

"Gar Wilson is excellent! Raw action attacks the reader on every page."

—*Don Pendleton*

Phoenix Force titles are available wherever paperbacks are sold.

GOLD
EAGLE

You don't know wha
NONSTOP
HIGH-VOLTAGI
ACTION
is until
you've read your
4 FREE
GOLD EAGLE
NOVELS

LIMITED-TIME OFFER

Mail to **Gold Eagle Reader Service**

In the U.S.
2504 West Southern Ave.
Tempe, AZ 85282

In Canada
P.O. Box 2800, Station A
5170 Yonge St.,
Willowdale, Ont. M2N 6J3

YEAH! Rush me 4 free Gold Eagle novels and my free mystery bonus. Then send me 6 brand-new novels every other month as they come off the presses. Bill me at the low price of $2.25 each— a 10% saving off the retail price. There are no shipping, handling or other hidden costs. There is no minimum number of books I must buy. I can always return a shipment and cancel at any time. Even if I never buy another book from Gold Eagle, the 4 free novels and the mystery bonus are mine to keep forever.

_____

Name   (PLEASE PRINT)

_____

Address   Apt. No.

_____

City   State/Prov.   Zip/Postal Code

_____

Signature (If under 18, parent or guardian must sign)

This offer is limited to one order per household and not valid to present subscribers. Price is subject to change.   166-BPM-BPGE

MYSTERY
BONUS GIF
HV–SUB–1